"Oh, Christine"

he said. "We didn't get off to a very good start, did we?"

"Look, Mark," she said softly, "I've met men like you before—men who want to play games. And the point is, I'm not interested. You told me that you don't want to get involved. Fine. I don't, either. And I don't want to engage in some meaningless little affair to gratify your ego."

"Is that what you think I want?"

She turned to move away, but she was off balance and fell straight into his arms.

"Ah, Christine," he said, grinning down as he held her close. "Was that intentional?"

APRIL THORNE

lives in northern California with her husband and several horses. They both enjoy travelling, but she's always glad to get home and start another book.

Dear Reader,

Silhouette Special Editions are an exciting new line of contemporary romances from Silhouette Books. Special Editions are written specifically for our readers who want a story with greater romantic detail.

Special Editions have all the elements you've enjoyed in Silhouette Romances and *more*. These stories concentrate on romance in a longer, more realistic and sophisticated way, and they feature greater sensual detail.

I hope you enjoy this book and all the wonderful romances from Silhouette. We welcome any suggestions or comments and invite you to write to us at the address below.

Jane Nicholls
Silhouette Books
PO Box 177
Dunton Green
Sevenoaks
Kent
TN13 2YE

APRIL THORNE

Once and Forever

Silhouette

Special Edition

Published by Silhouette Books

Copyright © 1982 by April Thorne

Map by Ray Lundgren

First printing 1983

British Library C.I.P.

Thorne, April
   Once and forever.—(Silhouette special edition)
   I. Title
   813'.54[F]   PS3570.H/

   ISBN 0 340 33355 3

Printed and bound in Great Britain for
Hodder and Stoughton Paperbacks, a
division of Hodder and Stoughton Ltd.,
Mill Road, Dunton Green, Sevenoaks,
Kent (Editorial Office: 47 Bedford
Square, London, WC1 3DP) by
Richard Clay (The Chaucer Press) Ltd.,
Bungay, Suffolk

Once and
Forever

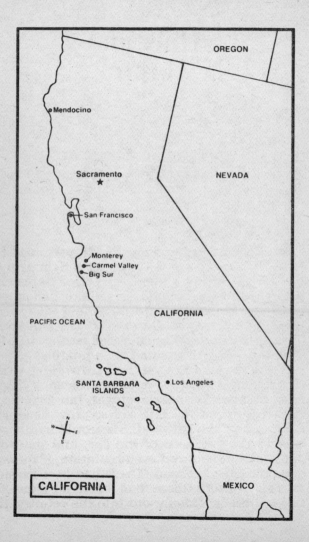

Chapter One

The Porsche skidded on the slippery road before Christine Winters could get a tight grip on the wheel. Fighting panic, she tried to remember to turn in the direction of the skid and prayed until the tires grabbed the pavement safely once more. "One for the Germans," she muttered, blessing Teutonic efficiency and letting out with a rush the breath she had been holding.

She peered out beyond the hardworking windshield wipers into the pitch dark ahead, trying to be calm after her near accident, but torrents of rain continued to fall across the headlight beams, and she frowned. She could hardly see beyond the low hood of the car, and she wondered again, with renewed irritation, if she was even on the right road. There had been no sign on this turnoff; there had been no signs for miles, in fact. This far out into the country, the only markers were half fallen into the ditches; impossible to read, where she couldn't even see them. Anya had told her that she and her husband, Peter, had replaced the carved sign for Wheel House Inn, but Christine hadn't seen that, either. Now she realized that if she didn't find something soon, a light or a landmark she recognized after all this time away, she would have to go back to the main highway and start over again. The prospect was depressing, and her temper was definitely not improved by the thought.

She was just reaching for the radio, thinking that the noise would at least be company, when there was a sudden jolt, a series of thumping noises, and then a steady bump . . . bump . . . bump. . . . The car jerked forward, the wheel shuddering under her hands, and she thought in a panic that she had hit something—some animal crossing the road in this accursed rain, too small for her to see in time, hidden by the storm. Cautiously she slowed the car even more, praying that she wouldn't have to get out and deal with some poor mangled little body. Then she realized that it hadn't been an animal after all: the car had a flat tire.

Jerking the key ring from the ignition, she sat back and tried not to burst into tears. The only sounds were the creaking of the car, the hard pounding of the rain against the roof, and the agitated drumming of her fingers against the steering wheel as she tried to control both tears and temper.

Did she remember how to change a flat tire? Had she ever known? Could she manage a jack on this muddy road, in the middle of the night, in the pouring rain? Of course she could, she thought angrily; changing a flat tire wasn't some ritual only men understood. It wasn't complicated, just messy and dirty and a bother.

"And I really don't need this right now," she muttered, glancing out the side window at the rain, wincing at the idea of getting out of the dry interior into the chilly, stormy night.

Biting her lip, Christine put her head back against the seat and thought childishly how unfair it all was. She was exhausted, worn out from the events of the past few weeks, and she didn't have the energy to cope with this maddening development; it was too much to ask after all that had happened.

Closing her eyes, she sighed heavily. Even in the faint light from the dashboard, and with a scarf tied around her head, she was a beautiful young woman. Her face, with only a trace of makeup, was the face of a fashion model, with wide-set green eyes and high cheekbones, a full mouth with a slightly pouting underlip, a straight nose, and a determined chin. Underneath the scarf, Christine's shoulder-length hair was true California: all shadings of blond, from ash to pale silver, highlighted by streaks of gold that gave it a lustrous sheen, like a fall of rich silk. Her dark brows and thick black lashes were natural, and contrasted startlingly with her fair complexion. Had she wanted to, she could have successfully earned a living in high fashion, for with her face and her tall, slender figure that looked equally stunning in jeans or evening dress, she might have been a top model. Many women had admired her appearance, most had been a little envious, and some even resented her a little. Christine was always surprised at such reactions; she knew she was lucky to look the way she did, but she had never dwelled on it. In fact, she had often thought impatiently that her appearance was a liability. Jealous women had a tendency to view her as competition; men had an irritating habit of seeing her as just a face and a body.

It had annoyed her all her twenty-eight years to be judged only on her looks, and she knew that was why she had deliberately spurned a modeling career for a profession that challenged her mind and talent and creativity.

She had majored in English in college, thinking vaguely as a freshman that she wanted to be a teacher. But her first course in creative writing had changed all that, opening up the exciting possibility of becoming a writer instead. From that point on, Christine had pursued a career in journalism with the same single-minded determination that had colored every major decision she had ever made. But it had been chance that directed her into the advertising field, and as she sat there in the car in the pouring rain Christine smiled bitterly.

She had been so excited when she landed that secretarial job in her first agency when she was still in college. It had been part of a work-study program, and she had seized the opportunity eagerly, anxious to see at first hand the working world of advertising, where so much depended on a clever turn of phrase, and where the introduction of a single catchword had the power to sell millions of dollars' worth of products. She had been in her third year of college then, avid to explore every facet of a writing career before she decided which field she would choose herself. She had never dreamed that advertising would become that career, and now, reflecting on it so long after that first secretarial job, Christine thought how different her life might have been if she had never walked through the door of McLean and Sullivan Advertising. How different, and how much easier. If she hadn't been so ambitious, she wouldn't be in the mess she was in now.

And she was in a mess, she admitted grimly. After eight long years of working her way up through the ranks at the agency, she was out of a job, she had no prospects of another one, and she wasn't even sure she wanted to continue in the field of advertising if something else came up.

And it was all, Christine thought with a bitter twist of her lips, because of Camilla Hall. Camilla, her own secretary—the girl who had taken the place Christine herself had occupied eight years before. Camilla, who wasn't above spreading lies and vicious gossip about Christine's sleeping her way to the top.

Christine had been incredulous at first when she heard the whispers about her supposed affair with Rob Sullivan, partner in McLean and Sullivan, and creative director of Christine's own department. She hadn't known whether to be scornful or amused at the rumors, or both. The gossip had started just the month before, when Christine had been promoted from senior copywriter to creative group head, second in command only to Rob Sullivan, and she had thought that it was just sour grapes—someone jealous of her promotion, and expressing that envy by slurring her reputation. She hadn't dreamed that anyone would take it seriously— after all, she had spent eight years working her way up to the position, and she deserved it after all the long overtime and the dedication she had brought to every job she had undertaken. She knew what she was doing at the agency, and what was more, she was good at her job. It showed, in the ad campaigns she had handled herself, in the accounts she had landed because of her creativity and hard work.

And now, because Camilla's ambition outran her sense of ethics, Christine's own career lay in ruins, while Camilla's star was rising.

Squirming inwardly, Christine admitted that she had no one to blame but herself. She should have seen it coming, she told herself; she should have recognized that behind Camilla's sweet, eager-to-please demeanor lurked a jackal in disguise. "Yes, Miss Winters," "No, Miss Winters," "Do you think I should retype this, Miss Winters?" Oh, Camilla had been so demure, so anxious to do whatever Christine wanted. What an innocent she had been! She should have known that behind those black eyes and smiling mouth was a determination to get Christine's job, in whatever way she could!

Grimacing at how neatly she had been fooled, Christine couldn't help remembering, too, that hideous scene in Richard McLean's office the day she resigned. She had been over it a hundred times in her mind since then, and she still winced whenever she thought about it. How she had managed to retain any poise or composure at all, she didn't know; she was just grateful at this point that she hadn't made a total fool of herself.

She could hear Richard McLean's solemn voice even now, the sonorous words rolling over her as she sat in the chair before his desk. Words like "affair," and "indiscreet," and "so disappointed in you," and, worst of all, "resignation."

One of the most difficult things she had ever done was to hold her head high and look McLean directly in the eyes. She had wanted to leap out of the chair and lean over the desk, screaming her innocence, pounding her fist on the polished wood to emphasize the point. But she had forced herself to sit quietly, calmly, she hoped, telling herself that a dignified silence was her best weapon.

Unfortunately, it turned out that she had no weapons at all. Richard McLean, it seemed, not only believed the malicious gossip; he actually condemned her without giving her a chance to defend herself against it. Even now, Christine could feel the same numb incredulity she had experienced then as he related the "facts" about the back-door love affair she was supposed to be having with his partner. She recalled the utter disbelief she had felt at the thought that he really believed she would offer herself in return for a promotion. She remembered that she had just stared at him for the first few awful minutes, unable to accept that he was really talking about her. She had thought—she had actually thought—that he had called her into his office to tell her that the gossip was just as distasteful and repugnant to him as it must be to her, and that he was going to make every effort to discover who had started the rumor and then fire the person responsible. Instead, he was sitting there with a righteous expression on his face, telling her that she must resign.

Somehow she had managed to find her voice. She had interrupted him, finally, as he was droning on about the image of the company, and she had said clearly, "I don't know what you're talking about, Mr. McLean."

He had stared at her. "I see," he said at last. "Well, I suppose I can't blame you for trying to deny it."

By some miracle, she had held on to her self-control. "I'm not trying to deny it, Mr. McLean; I *am* denying it! Rob Sullivan and I have never had an affair; nor do we anticipate having one. My God! The man is married!"

She had sat back then, armed, she thought, with her innocence. She was proud of herself for holding on to her temper, proud that she hadn't become hysterical or burst into furious tears, or done something else equally humiliating. She waited for his apology. It never came.

Richard McLean frowned. "The fact that a man is married," he said heavily, "is sometimes not a consideration."

It was Christine's turn to stare at him. A hundred things crossed her mind to say to him, and she rejected them all in the space of an instant. Finally she managed to say, with dignity, "It is a consideration with me. But that is really beside the point, I think. I don't believe in advancing my career in such a despicable fashion, whatever you may think. I've always made it a practice to keep my private life separate from my business life, and I will continue to do so, if only to avoid the inevitable complications. I thought you knew that, Mr. McLean. I've been with your company for eight years; you yourself supported my promotion to group head. How can you possibly believe—"

She had to stop for a minute. Her voice was starting to shake, and she knew she had to cut this short before she became too angry to continue. "If you're so willing to believe this . . . this vicious slander, then perhaps we would both be happier if I worked elsewhere."

She had expected him to offer an apology then, to ask her to stay, to tell her that it had all been a monstrous mistake and that he was convinced of her innocence. He did none of those things. Incredulous, she watched him nod solemnly. "Yes," he said. "Perhaps that would be best, Miss Winters."

Painted into a corner, she was helpless to retract her own rash resignation. Somehow she managed to get to her feet with a little dignity, and her head was high when she said in parting, "You'll have my letter of resignation this afternoon, Mr. McLean. But I do wonder one thing. . . ."

"Yes?"

Her hand was on the doorknob. She turned to stare directly at him. "I wonder," she said clearly, "if you asked Mr. Sullivan about this supposed liaison."

He didn't have to answer; the look on his face

was enough. "No," she said quietly. "I thought not. Well, somehow, it doesn't surprise me."

She had left the office then, without waiting to hear McLean's reply, and she had met Camilla in the hall. The girl's black eyes were no longer demure but slanted with malice, and Camilla's sweet expression had become sly. Christine had known, then, who was responsible for starting the rumors, and for a long minute the two women just stared at each other. All the noise and bustle and hurry of a typical day at the agency swirled around them; with part of her mind, Christine could hear the Accounting Service fussing over an ad budget, and in another office the Media Department was engaged in an argument about the best way to present some new product. One of the paste-up girls rushed by on the way to Research, and an office boy staggered past, loaded down with a stack of tapes from Print Production. Frenzied activity was going on all around her, but Christine saw only Camilla. She walked toward her, ignoring all the confusion surrounding them. They could have been alone in the hall.

"Advertising is a tough, competitive world," Christine said softly as she came up to Camilla. "But I suspect that you knew that before you came. You were a tough competitor before you walked in the door, weren't you?"

Camilla's eyes were hard and black, almost glittering, as she stared defiantly at Christine. "My father was a military man," she said, her mouth a tight, ugly line. "And he used to tell me this: 'Take the high ground, or they'll bury you in the valley.' I wasn't going to be buried in a dead-end secretary job, that's all. No one ever gave me anything, Christine; I learned early that if I wanted something, I had to take it."

"No one ever gave me anything, either, Camilla. But—"

"Oh, don't give me that!" Camilla sneered. "You have it all! Looks, brains—talent. You're the golden girl, don't you know? Or you were, I should say. Because there's something you don't have, after all. As my old man would say, you don't have the killer instinct."

"And you do."

"Yes," Camilla admitted aggressively. "I do. And that's why I'm going to get ahead."

Christine had been furious before; now, seeing that fierce look in Camilla's eyes, she felt only pity for the girl. "I see," she said quietly. "Well, I hope you get what you want. Unfortunately for you, it won't be my job—not for a while, if ever. You don't have the experience or, I'm afraid, the talent. And you certainly have a lot to learn about dealing with people." Camilla's eyes were bright, furious, at that, but Christine ignored the murderous glare Camilla threw at her. "And just remember one thing," she added.

"And what is that?" Camilla ground out, livid.

"Just remember that the high ground you spoke so fondly of is sometimes just another hill that no one else cares about. Sometimes the sacrifices you make taking it aren't worth the pile of dirt you're left with."

Christine had walked away then, leaving Camilla staring after her, speechless with rage. She didn't care. She had gone straight to her office, typed out a letter of resignation, left her keys on the desk, and gone home. The goodbyes to the people at the agency had come later, when she could face her friends with a little composure; but for a week she had moped around her apartment in Sausalito, alternately raging at the injustice of it and crying at the idea of losing her job. It didn't matter at that point that she had resigned instead of letting McLean fire her; the fact remained that she had been forced to leave because of an archaic double standard embraced by a man who still lived in the Dark Ages. It wasn't fair; she had been tried, convicted, and condemned without cause, and if she had been a man, none of it would have happened.

At the end of the week, Rob Sullivan came to see her, and Christine, who had finally managed to get her feelings somewhat under control, was infuriated all over again. If the scene with Richard McLean had been distasteful, the visit by Rob Sullivan to her apartment was even worse. She couldn't believe it when, after she had invited him in, he told her he had called a meeting of all the department directors to deny the rumors about him and Christine.

"You did *what?*" she had cried, appalled.

"Well, I had to do something," he replied comfortably, sipping the drink she had made for him. "I couldn't just sit by and let you be accused of something like that."

She wanted to point out acidly that if she had been accused, so had he. After all, they *were* supposed to have engaged in a sordid affair, and she could hardly have been guilty by herself.

Instead, she took a deep breath and asked, "And what was the outcome of this . . . this conference?"

She had once thought that Rob Sullivan was a handsome man. Tonight he wore a dark business suit, carefully tailored to show off the physique he was so proud of, in a rich blue color that contrasted deliberately with his blond good looks. He was lean, lithe from hours of racquetball, tanned from afternoons of tennis, boyish and bright, and very good at his job as creative director of the agency. He was Richard McLean's partner, but he had shunned the responsibilities and details of a vice-presidency in the company, preferring to work directly with clients and his staff. Christine, in her own position as senior copywriter, had worked directly with him for the past five years, and together they had managed many successful ad campaigns. She had enjoyed working with him; she had learned a lot from him; and she had admired and respected him. She had even, she admitted uncomfortably, been attracted to him. Once. But not tonight. Tonight she saw him in a new light, and she didn't like what she saw. Infuriated, she watched Rob try to hide a superior male smile that held both pity and pride, and she wondered what had ever attracted her to him. He was actually *proud* to think that everyone would believe they had had an affair; he actually had the gall to pity her. It was too much.

"Never mind," she said abruptly, setting down her own untouched glass. "I don't really want to know, after all."

She stood and walked purposefully to the door. Rob had no choice but to follow her, but he paused before he went out. "I'm really sorry about all this," he said sincerely. "Are you sure you won't . . . reconsider?"

"Reconsider what?" she asked coldly.

"Well . . . Richard feels that he might have acted a little hastily. He's very conservative, as you know, and yet, in all fairness, he thinks that you deserve another chance."

Another chance! Christine bit back a sharp response to that and said instead, "It's a bit late for that, don't you think? And what's more, I don't think *he* deserves another chance." She shook her head. "No, Rob; I'm not coming back. I just couldn't work for a man who was so eager to believe something like that about me. It's too late for amends, whatever Richard McLean thinks."

Rob's expression was regretful. "I'm sorry you feel that way, Christine. We worked well together, you and I. And the agency is really going to miss you—Richard, too," he added solemnly.

"Perhaps he should have thought of that before he called me into his office."

Rob hesitated. Christine's hand was on the doorknob; she was obviously anxious for him to leave. "I thought you might like to know—"

"What?"

"I fired Camilla Hall today. It . . . it seemed the least I could do."

Christine thought of Camilla's hard black eyes and sly expression, and didn't feel sorry for her. If she hadn't made it at McLean and Sullivan, she would make it somewhere else; Christine was sure of that. The killer instinct. Camilla had it in spades, she thought. She wouldn't be out of a job for long.

"Well . . ." Rob was uncomfortable. Awkwardly he patted Christine on the arm. "If you need a reference or a letter of recommendation, don't hesitate to ask. And if you do reconsider, the agency would be glad to have you back. I mean that, Christine—really."

"Thank you, Rob. But I'm not sure I even want to continue in advertising, after this."

Rob was surprised. "You don't mean that! Why, you're one of the best copywriters we had!"

"There are . . . other things," she said vaguely, wishing he would go. She looked at him, at the blue eyes that seemed so candid and sincere, and she was unmoved. "Thank you for coming to see me, Rob," she said. She managed a smile. "Who knows? All this might have been for the best. Maybe it's time to move on to something else."

Rob had left then, unconvinced, and as Christine shut the door she wondered why she had dredged up that inane platitude. Had she said it only to get rid of him, or was it something else? Was she secretly relieved to be gone from the agency—from advertising?

Gingerly she had examined the thought. She had spent eight years in the advertising field, after all; was she eager to give it up, or reluctant?

Even now, a week after Rob's visit, sitting in her car in the rain, Christine didn't know. She still wasn't sure what she wanted to do about her career; the only thing she was sure of, she thought grimly, glancing at the streaming car window, was that she had to do something about that stupid flat tire. Sighing, she reached for the door handle.

There was a fresh gust of rain the moment she stepped outside, and Christine exclaimed in annoyance as a cold trickle of water dampened the inside of her collar. Her boots were covered with mud by the time she managed to feel her way to the back of the car in the darkness, and when she looked down, she saw that the soft leather was ruined. Lips tight, she untied the now sodden silk scarf that had covered her hair and stuffed it into a pocket before she inserted the key into the back lock of the car.

For once, the smooth hydraulic lift of the back window refused to engage, and she struggled with the key, wondering blackly why she had splurged on the Porsche when it was obvious that she should have settled for something sensible—like a Volkswagen. Fighting the urge to smash the expensive window with her fist, Christine took a deep breath, reinserted the key, and hoped that it would open this time the way it should. It did.

She was bending over the trunk, trying to lift out the heavy spare and wondering how she was ever going to change the tire when she could barely lift the thing, when a flash of lights from behind her made her straighten abruptly. She was not normally a fearful young woman, but her heart lurched at the slow approach of another car, and she tried to calm herself by remembering the self-defense class she had taken some time ago for just such an emergency.

She couldn't remember a thing. Groaning, the only thing she could recall was her mother's advice, floating to her from years back, as other mothers' voices had spoken sternly to thousands of other little girls: "Scream, dear—and don't be afraid to kick, as hard as you can."

Yes, she thought scathingly; she supposed that would work very well in oxfords. But what, she wondered darkly, did one do in high-heeled boots on a slippery, muddy country road that was pitch black, and miles from any recognizable civilization?

She felt impaled by the lights from the other car as it slowly approached, and she was suddenly all too aware of the defenseless picture she made: her hair scraggling wetly over her shoulders, her drenched and sodden coat, her muddy boots, and her awkward position as she balanced the heavy spare on the bumper of the car. She wished abruptly that she had found the jack before the car came; she would have felt much more secure with a heavy piece of metal in her hand, whether she could have used it or not.

The car slowed, the driver obviously hesitating between stopping altogether and going around her. Christine herself alternated between hoping that whoever it was would help and willing the car to go on, leaving her to struggle alone. She was very aware of the isolated road, the darkness, and the fact that the only person besides Anya who knew where she was going was a friend in the city, Phyllis. Christine hadn't wanted anyone else, even her sister Carla, to know that she was retreating to Wheel House Inn. A working vacation, Anya had laughed when she begged Christine to come, and Christine had convinced herself that that was exactly what it was.

The car was coming to a stop, and Christine saw with mixed relief and fear that the driver was a man. She wasn't reassured about him when, instead of rolling the window down to ask if she needed any help, he turned off the ignition and jerked open his car door.

"You might at least have pulled over to the side of the road," the stranger shouted as he struggled into a jacket. "You don't even have the flashers on—I might have hit you!"

Christine's fear evaporated in a rush of anger. She was tired, worn out from the past two weeks, annoyed about the flat and the rain, and trying to fight the sinking feeling that she was lost. She didn't need any criticism from this man, whoever he was.

"I didn't think I would need flashers on this godforsaken road," she snapped as he came up to her. "There hasn't been another car for miles!"

"Here—give me that." As if she hadn't spoken, he took the spare from her and bounced it down impatiently to the ground, balancing it easily and making her feel ridiculous for having tried to hold it on the bumper.

"Would you like some help?" he asked nastily. "Or are you one of those liberated women who have to prove they can do everything themselves?"

Christine just prevented herself from grabbing the tire. She could picture herself struggling with the flat, the jack, and the lug nuts—or whatever they were—in this wretched rain while this rude man laughed at her, and for once common sense prevailed over pride.

"I would be out of my mind to refuse such a gracious offer," she retorted sarcastically.

He grunted, and in the darkness Christine couldn't tell if the sound was a laugh or a sign of annoyance. Ignoring her again, he reached forward into the trunk and grabbed the tools he needed. "Which one is it?"

"The left rear," she answered shortly. "I have a flashlight. Would you like me to get it?"

"That might be a help."

She flushed at the sarcastic note in his voice, and her lips tightened as she went to get the flashlight from the glove compartment. Of all the men who might have come along to help her, she thought angrily, she had to find one who hated women. Would this hideous night ever end?

By the time she returned, the man had wheeled the spare around to the left side and was struggling with the flat. He began changing the tire in silence, and as Christine held the light for him and watched she realized with chagrin that she could never have managed it herself. As strong as he was, he had trouble with it, and she wondered how she could have done it alone. For the first time she was really grateful that he had stopped, and yet, when she swallowed her pride and tried to tell him so, he only grunted again. She gave up, irritated. Did he have to be so rude?

The rain poured down, chilling her through to the skin as he worked, and she shifted from one foot to the other, trying not to shiver in the cold. She was miserable, and what was more, she thought with a sinking feeling, she didn't even know how far it was to Wheel House.

She must have been crazy, she decided, transferring the flashlight to her other hand, to listen to Anya telling her it would do her good, getting away to a remote country inn to take her mind off her troubles. How had she let Anya talk her into such a harebrained idea, anyway? What had seemed such a great notion at the time now took on nerve-racking proportions, especially since it was too late to back out of her promise. It was hard to believe that she had agreed, not only to come to Wheel House for a visit but to take care of the place while Anya and Peter were gone. She must have been out of her mind to listen to Anya's persuasiveness, and yet she could hear even now her friend's bright, cheerful, insistent voice when she had called, the same night Rob Sullivan had come to see her at her apartment.

Typically, Anya had called at two in the morning. The phone had shrilled suddenly in the quiet darkness, and Christine had jumped, spilling a few drops of a glass of wine she had been holding while she stared blankly out at the lights across the bay. San Francisco. The city where she no longer worked.

"Chris—is that you?"

Christine knew who it was at once, even though it had been months since she had heard Anya's voice. She and Anya Lyle had been friends since college days when they had been roommates, and Anya had been the only person ever to call her Chris.

"Chris?"

"Yes, I'm here. Anya—do you know what time it is?"

There was a pause. "No. Why? Oh—is it late?"

Christine had to laugh. She had often wondered how she and Anya had managed to stay friends, for they were exact opposites. Where Christine was meticulous and responsible and dependable, Anya was frivolous and irrepressible and totally unreliable—except in her loyalty to her friends. She was scatterbrained and untidy, and never remembered where things were. Her closets were jumbled, her dresser drawers a horror, and yet somehow the bills were always paid, and Anya always had a smile. Christine was often impatient with her friend's untidy life, but she had never disliked her for traits that would have maddened her in anyone else. Anya was simply . . . Anya, with frizzy hair and unmatched clothes—and underneath that helpless and appealing manner was a sharp mind and a shrewd intelligence that she tried so hard to hide. It was all an act—that scatterbrained, running-around-in-circles demeanor that Anya cultivated—just as Christine's own manner was an act in her own way. She tried to project the image of a confident, competent, liberated woman of the eighties, and yet sometimes Christine had to admit that she didn't want to be so darned capable. It would be wonderful, she would think wistfully, to lean on someone else for a change, to let down her guard and reveal

the other, more vulnerable side of her nature—
the hidden part that didn't mind being loved and
pampered and spoiled . . . occasionally. As a
constant diet, Christine rejected the idea of
dependence, but still, there were times . . .

"Chris?"

Christine started. "I'm sorry, Anya. What were
you saying?"

"I don't blame you for being preoccupied.
You've been through a lot these past weeks,
haven't you?"

Christine winced. "Don't tell me you've heard
about it, all the way at the back of beyond." Anya
and her husband, Peter, owned a country inn on
the coast, about a hundred miles north of San
Francisco.

"We aren't completely isolated from civilization," Anya said airily. "We do have a telephone,
you know, when we get tired of using smoke
signals!"

"Phyllis told you, didn't she?" Christine demanded. Despite Anya's isolation in the north
country, as she called it, she and Phyllis and
Christine, who had known each other since
school, had kept up their friendship. "Didn't
she?" Christine asked again.

"Well . . . yes," Anya admitted. "And that's
really why I called—"

"Oh, not to talk about the *grande passion* that
was supposed to have taken place! Not you, too!"

"Come on—what do you take me for, anyway?
Some common gossip hound who doesn't have
anything better to do? You know better than
that, Chris. I'm not interested in whether you

had an affair or not. We're big girls now, aren't we? Whose business is it, anyway?"

Christine grimaced. "Apparently, everyone at McLean and Sullivan."

"Oh, who cares about a bunch of small-minded people?" With a sniff, Anya dismissed the ad agency. "I don't want to talk about that, in any case. I called about something else."

Christine was accustomed to these quick conversational changes with Anya. "All right; let's not talk about it. What did you call about?"

For the first time, Anya was silent. It was so unlike her to hesitate that Christine frowned. "Anya?"

"Chris—I have a favor to ask you. A big favor."

"All right. What is it?"

"Just like that?"

"Yes, just like that," Christine replied dryly. "What is it?"

"Well, you might not be so agreeable when you hear—"

"*What*, for goodness' sake?"

Anya paused again. Finally, she said in a small voice, "I wouldn't ask you, Christine, but there's no one else I would trust. Do you . . . do you think you could come up here for a few weeks, to sort of . . . sort of take care of the inn?"

"*What?*"

"Look," Anya said hurriedly, "I know it's a big thing to ask, but I'm desperate, Chris—really."

"Anya, is something wrong?"

There was another pause, and this time, to Christine's astonishment, she could hear Anya's voice catch. Anya rarely cried; she was more likely to laugh about problems, no matter how big or small. It was her defense . . . her act.

"Anya?"

"It's Peter, Chris—" Peter was Anya's husband, a small, intense man who had had drinking problems in the past. He had been an artist at one time, but he hadn't touched a brush in years; his hands had trembled too much when he drank, and when he had finally managed to conquer his alcoholism, he had lost confidence in himself as an artist. That was when Anya had talked him into buying the Wheel House, a battered old Victorian she had found on California's north coast. It had once been used as a spectacular guest house for a lumber company, but it had gradually been allowed to sink into ruin. Built in the late 1800s, with two cottages added to the property around the 1920s, the house had been a real find—for someone who had the time and the talent and the funds to convert it into a popular country inn. Anya had given up her own thriving book and record store to back the new venture, and at first the Lyles had been a smashing success. They had owned the mortgage on Wheel House for four years now, and as far as Christine knew, the inn had never lacked for guests.

"What's wrong with Peter, Anya?" Christine asked quietly.

"He's . . . he's . . . ." Despite her efforts, Anya's voice broke again. "He's drinking, Chris."

"Oh, no!"

"Oh, yes." Anya was grim now. "And I have to get him away for a while, the doctor says. He thinks it's the pressure of having Wheel House that started it."

"But the inn has always been such a success! What kind of pressure are you talking about?"

"Well . . . we haven't been doing so well this past year."

"Why didn't you say something?"

"Oh, sure! What was I going to say? That my husband was falling apart right before my eyes? And that Wheel House was, too, because I was so involved in what was happening with Peter? Oh, look—it doesn't matter now, does it? The important thing is that the doctor says there's a new clinic he wants Peter to go to. It's in Los Angeles, and they've had wonderful results detoxifying . . . alcoholics. We have an appointment after waiting a long time for it, but I can't leave this place without knowing that it will be taken care of."

"But, Anya—I don't know anything about running an inn!"

"Neither did I when I started." For the first time since they had begun talking about Peter, Anya's voice took on a hint of laughter. "It's a sort of trial-and-error thing, anyway, Chris—you can't possibly do as badly as I did those first few months. And we won't be gone that long—just a couple of weeks."

"A couple of weeks! But—"

"And Mrs. Mallory will be here to oversee things—"

"Who's Mrs. Mallory?"

"Oh, she's the housekeeper; she keeps track of the maids and the linens and things," Anya answered vaguely.

"Then why can't she take over for a while?"

"Well, she could, I suppose. In fact, knowing Mrs. Mallory, she could probably run the entire establishment much better than I ever could."

"Well, then?"

"Chris, this is my life—mine and Peter's. I just can't leave it to a stranger, no matter how competent she is. Can't you understand?"

Christine could. She could also hear the underlying note of desperation in Anya's voice, no matter how she tried to hide it. It was so unlike Anya that Christine knew the trouble went far deeper than her friend was willing to confess, even to her. How could she let her down now?

"All right," Christine said, sighing. "I'll try. But don't blame me," she added gloomily, "if everything goes wrong and you come back to complete chaos."

"Oh, that won't happen," Anya replied with assurance. "I know you, Chris—nothing you touched would dare go wrong. You always have such confidence!"

But she had no confidence now, waiting for this stranger to finish changing the flat so she could climb wearily back into her car and try to find her way to Wheel House. And getting there was only part of the problem, she thought ruefully; taking charge of the place once she found it was something else entirely. What had ever made her think she could manage a country inn? What had ever convinced Anya that she could? She didn't know anything about running a hostelry; she would have had more success designing a skyscraper! At this point, it didn't even cheer Christine to remember that Anya had promised to be there until tomorrow to answer Christine's questions, and that she had agreed to leave copious notes. Christine was used to Anya's heartfelt promises, and her heart sank when she pictured how it would really go: explanations given by Anya on the run, the promised notes somehow never written.

And yet . . . wasn't this, nerve-racking as it was, better than sitting in her empty apartment, contemplating the ruin of a promising career, and wondering what she was going to do next?

"That's it."

With another grunt, the man stood. There was a smear of mud across his face, but Christine didn't dare tell him about it; his expression was fierce enough to silence her. It was an effort for her to say, "I don't know how to thank you—"

"Don't, then," the man said rudely. "But next time, maybe you had better have your mechanic —if you have one—check the car before you take a trip. It seems a reasonable precaution, I'd think."

She was in no mood to listen to a lecture on auto safety. Stung by the criticism, she nodded curtly and then watched in silence as he stowed the tools and the flat in the trunk. He was a tall man, broad-shouldered and strong, for he handled the heavy items with ease. As he straightened again and his profile was outlined in the glare from the headlights of his car behind them Christine saw that while he wasn't conventionally handsome, he was very good-looking in his own way: thick, dark hair, a hard jaw, a slightly hooked nose, a wide mouth, and deep-set dark eyes under heavy brows. He wore his clothes well—jeans and boots, Irish cable sweater under the jacket—and Christine flushed in the darkness when he turned toward her and she realized that she had been staring at him, intrigued.

"Well," she said awkwardly when he slammed the hatch down and held out the key to her, "I do appreciate your help."

"Think nothing of it," he answered, and strode away to his own car.

She looked after him, her mouth open with surprise. He might at least have waited until she was safely inside her car, she thought in annoyance. But then, she should consider herself lucky that he had stopped at all. She would still be struggling with the heavy spare tire if he hadn't come along, and as she moved to open the car door she shrugged. Despite the fact that he had helped her, he had been curt and rude, and she decided that she didn't like him at all.

They hadn't even introduced themselves, she realized, watching in the rearview mirror as he pulled away from the roadside and went around her. And that was fine, too. The encounter with him had been totally unpleasant, and she would never see him again.

Yet, as she drove away herself, she was still thinking of the stranger. It was rare that she disliked someone she didn't even know, but she hadn't cared for this man at all, despite his good looks and his fierce, compelling eyes. She didn't like dark-haired men, anyway, she told herself. Then she remembered that Rob Sullivan was blond, and she frowned. She had been attracted to him once, but nothing had come of it. She hadn't lied to Richard McLean when she denied having an affair with Rob; there had been nothing going on between them except business. Period. Her conscience was clear on that score, thank God.

The rain seemed to have abated slightly, and Christine didn't have to concentrate so hard on her driving. That was unfortunate, because now she had too much time to think of other things, and, inevitably, she thought of the agency and her work there. She had been so proud, only a month ago, when her promotion had come through. She had worked hard for it, and it had been another step toward her ultimate goal of a vice-presidency. But now . . . now she knew how easily dreams could be destroyed. She knew she would have been good at her new job as creative group head; she had the knowledge and the ability to direct the copywriters and art directors under her, and because they respected her as much as she did them, they could have worked well together. She would even have been able to do some writing herself, if she chose. It would have been the best of both worlds—until the next promotion. And the one after that. Oh, she had had it all planned—until that disastrous scene with Richard McLean. Now she wasn't even sure she wanted to continue in advertising.

That was the problem, Christine mused. Did she want to continue? She knew she could easily get another job at a different agency; she had the qualifications, even without a reference from McLean and Sullivan. And she had once loved her work, despite the nature of advertising. It could be a rough world, and a real rat race, and there were things about it that repelled her and made her less than proud of her profession. But she had never used some of the techniques available, such as subliminal advertising, using sex or sexuality to promote a product, or manipulating underlying fears or phobias hidden from consumers themselves to compel them to buy. She hadn't needed such leverage: she had believed, and still did, that cleverness and wit and pure talent could be used to better advantage.

She sighed. Perhaps she was really an innocent, as Camilla seemed to believe. Maybe she wouldn't have made it in a larger agency, in the fiercely competitive Madison Avenue style. She didn't know at this point. She supposed it really didn't matter now, anyway. McLean and Sullivan was part of her past—a part she wanted to forget while she tried to decide what to do next.

Thankfully, the gleam of lights ahead distracted her from her depressing thoughts, and she looked up eagerly, hoping that she had finally found Wheel House Inn.

Slowing, she came up to what she hoped was a sign. But the only object her headlights picked up was a post with a crossarm. The two eyebolts screwed into the bottom of the arm were empty, and Christine didn't know whether to laugh or be annoyed. Anya was right, she thought; someone was determined to steal the inn sign, whether it was bolted in or not.

But she didn't need to have a sign pointing the way now; she recognized the huge old Victorian house at the end of the drive. She had been here once before with Phyllis, when Anya and Peter had first bought the place and they had come to help celebrate. It had been too long ago, Christine thought as she turned into the driveway; she should have made the effort to visit Anya here before now. It was just that Anya, living in such isolation, liked to come to the city every once in a while, to get away, and Christine, always busy with her job, found it difficult to get away herself. It had been easier to invite Anya to visit her.

The house was lighted from top to bottom, she saw as she approached, and there were a few cars in the small parking lot hidden under the trees. To her surprise, there was a group of people in the entry when she opened the front door, and when they all turned to look at her, she was unnerved. What was it? Had something happened to Anya or Peter?

A woman detached herself from the cluster and came toward Christine, introducing herself at once as Mrs. Mallory, the housekeeper. Christine smiled, doing her best to ignore the tense atmosphere. "I'm Christine Winters," she said.

"I know; Anya described you perfectly," Mrs. Mallory replied with a warm smile. She hesitated. "I'm so glad you're here," she added. "There is a bit of a . . . problem."

Alarmed, Christine glanced at the small knot of people, then back to the housekeeper again. "What kind of problem? Is it Anya—or Peter?"

"Oh, no. I'm so sorry; I didn't mean to frighten you," Mrs. Mallory answered, seeing Christine's alarmed expression. She glanced around, realized that everyone was listening, and added in a low voice, "May I speak to you privately?"

"Of course."

They went to a room off the hall. When Mrs. Mallory opened the door, Christine realized that it must be Anya's office, for there was a desk piled high with papers, and ledgers and menus and receipts and books were scattered all over. Christine shut the door behind them. Trying to retain some composure, she asked, "What is it?"

Mrs. Mallory clasped her hands. She was, Christine thought absently, exactly the way she had pictured her. In her mid-fifties, it seemed, Mrs. Mallory had iron-gray hair swept back into a tight little bun on top of her round head. She was a big woman, and heavy; the flesh on her arms swung slightly with each movement, and her double chin was rapidly descending into a third. She was dressed in a dark print dress with a lace handkerchief tucked through her belt, and on her small feet were the most sensible of Red Cross shoes. But her blue eyes were kind and direct, and she seemed so capable that Christine believed that, whatever disaster had occurred, they could manage together. A few seconds later, she wasn't so sure.

"Anya asked me to tell you how sorry she was," Mrs. Mallory began apologetically, "but she and Peter had to leave today."

"Oh, no!" Christine had counted so much on Anya's being here to explain everything that she hadn't thought about what she would do if something had gone wrong and Anya wasn't at the inn when she arrived.

"She tried to call you this morning, but there was no answer," Mrs. Mallory continued. "And they couldn't stay. Their appointment was changed at the clinic, and they couldn't refuse to go after waiting for it so long."

"I understand," Christine said faintly. She pushed aside a stack of towels hiding one of the chairs. Sinking into it, she tried not to be dismayed at this unexpected crisis. "I don't suppose Anya remembered to leave me any written instructions," she said hopefully.

The housekeeper glanced around the cluttered office and lifted her hands in a gesture of defeat. "You're welcome to look," she offered.

Christine looked around, too, and then she sighed. "Knowing Anya, I doubt that it would do any good." Dredging up a smile, she said, "I guess I'll just have to do the best I can."

"I'll try to help, Miss Winters. I told Anya I would be willing to do what I could."

"Thank you," Christine said fervently. "I'll take you up on that, I'm afraid."

"Unfortunately, that's not all, Miss Winters. . . ."

Christine's sinking feeling plummeted another few notches. Abandoning her attempt at a smile, she said, "Call me Christine, please. And maybe you'd better let me have it all at once."

"All right, then," Mrs. Mallory said reluctantly. "But I hate to tell you all this the second you arrive. One of the maids quit this afternoon, and then . . . there's something the matter with the plumbing."

"The plumbing!" The maid's defection was ignored by Christine in the light of this particular disaster. She could always find someone to help with the housekeeping; she could lend a hand herself. But plumbing was different. She hadn't the faintest idea what to do about pipes and hot and cold water and drains and faucets. In fact, she realized with a wry desperation, the only thing she really knew about the intricacies of plumbing was that when she turned on the tap, water miraculously appeared.

"What's the matter with it?" Christine did her best to sound calm. She almost succeeded.

"I don't know," Mrs. Mallory said unhappily. "It's just that there's no hot water."

Christine groaned. Glancing at her watch, she saw that it was after ten, and she wondered what her chances were of talking a plumber into coming out this late. Assuming, she thought glumly, that there was a plumber to call. She didn't know how far away the nearest town was—or even if there was an emergency service there. Right now, she had never felt more incompetent and confused.

But Mrs. Mallory was looking expectantly at her, and she had to say something. Anya had left her in charge; she was depending on her, and Christine was supposed to have the ability to make quick decisions. That was why she had been so good at her job, she thought acidly; she hadn't been afraid to stick her neck out.

"Well," she said, more briskly than she felt. She got to her feet and went to Anya's untidy mess of a desk, hoping she could find something there to guide her. But if Anya had remembered to leave emergency numbers for her, they were buried under the avalanche, and Christine sighed. She should have known; she was going to have to handle this herself. Somehow.

"The first thing to do, I suppose, is to try to find

a plumber—or maybe a handyman who can fix pipes and things," she said finally as she turned back to the waiting housekeeper. "Maybe we can at least discover what's wrong with the water heater. The maid, I think, can wait until morning, can't she?" Christine looked at Mrs. Mallory, who nodded. "Good. I suppose dinner is over now, and the kitchen is closed for the night?" Another nod. "So we don't have to worry about food or service until tomorrow. How many guests are there?"

If Mrs. Mallory was surprised by Christine's abrupt air of authority, she didn't betray it. "Just two couples, right now—and a single," she answered readily.

"Have you explained about the hot water to them?"

"Well, I thought it best to say something."

"Good." That explained the milling about in the front hall. Christine took a deep breath. "I think I better go out, too, and tell them that we're working on fixing it, and doing the best we can. What do you think?"

Mrs. Mallory nodded admiringly. "I think that's a good idea," she said with a smile. "It's strange . . . I mean . . . Well, it's just that you're so different from—"

"From what you expected?"

"No—from Anya."

They both laughed, and then Christine said, "I don't think anyone in the world is like Anya. And at this point, I'm not sure whether to be grateful for that or not!"

She remembered suddenly that she still wore her dripping coat, and she shrugged out of it, hanging it on a hook behind the door before turning purposefully to the desk again. She began lifting papers and magazines and empty coffee cups, trying to find the phone.

"Do you have any idea where the phone book is, Mrs. Mallory?" Christine asked as she spied a cord. She followed it successfully to the telephone that was stuck behind a stack of books on a shelf over the desk. She seized it triumphantly. "Or maybe you already know a plumber I can call," she added.

Mrs. Mallory's silence was telling. Christine looked back at her, saw the housekeeper's unhappy expression, and sighed. "Don't tell me," she said. "There isn't anyone to call, right?"

"Well . . ."

"What would Anya do about this situation? She had to have someone who could fix things around here; Peter isn't interested in carpentry or anything like that, I know. What did Anya do when she needed someone to come out?"

"She had a handyman, someone from Mendocino. But . . ."

Christine closed her eyes. "But he isn't available," she finished. Of course he wasn't, she thought: Mrs. Mallory would have called him herself if he were.

Biting her lip, Christine tried to think what to do. It was obvious that she had to do something, for she couldn't expect the guests to be without hot water for long. A few hours might be an adventure; longer than that was a disaster.

"Mrs. Mallory, there must be someone who could—"

There was a sharp knock on the door just then, interrupting her. Before she could answer, the knob turned and a man stood in the doorway, lounging against the frame. When Christine recognized him, she was startled enough to exclaim, "What are you doing here?" It was the stranger who had helped her on the road.

Ignoring her, he glanced instead at the housekeeper. "Do you know there isn't any water?"

"Of course we know," Christine snapped before Mrs. Mallory could answer.

"'We'?" he asked lazily. "Are you the owner of the inn, or just another irate guest?"

"Miss Winters is taking over for the Lyles while they are away," the housekeeper said hastily. She glanced at Christine's angry face and added, "Mr. Harrison is one of our guests, Christine."

"Oh. I—see." Christine tried to hide her dismay at that information. "Well, I hope you enjoy your stay," she added, gritting her teeth. "And don't worry; there will be hot water again as soon as possible. You won't be put out much longer."

"You're not going to find anyone to fix the plumbing this late at night," Harrison said with a nasty smile in her direction, enjoying her discomfort. "Wheel House isn't really at the hub of civilization, is it?"

"I think we can manage, Mr. Harrison," Christine said stiffly. "But you will have to excuse us . . ."

Annoyed, she saw that he wasn't about to leave. In fact, she thought irately, he seemed to be amused at her predicament, for he was watching her with an evil gleam in his eyes. She turned abruptly away.

There was a phone book balanced precariously at the edge of the desk; she had found it when she was searching for the telephone. Now she seized the thin little book triumphantly, and with a hard glance at the smiling Mr. Harrison, she opened it to the plumbing section—or what was supposed to be the plumbing section. There was no entry between the headings of Plants and Pottery. She looked again—and again—under Appliance Repair and Water Supply, and had to accept finally that there was no help at all. Fighting the urge to throw the book across the cluttered room in a fury, Christine made herself put it carefully back on the littered desk instead.

Harrison had remained lounging against the door during Christine's frenetic search. Now he straightened and said casually, "I can have a look at the water heater, if you like."

Christine stared at him. He had let her fumble through that entire phone book, frantically looking for assistance, and he hadn't said a word until now? She could have dashed across the room and slapped him.

Mrs. Mallory saw Christine's expression and tried to excuse herself. Christine stopped her with a gesture, hoping to get control of her temper before she spoke to Mr. Harrison. She had been about to refuse his belated offer of assistance with a scathing remark, but now she realized that she would have to swallow her pride once again and accept his help. She had to think of the guests waiting for service; now was not the time to give in to a tantrum, no matter how tempting the thought.

"I'm afraid I'll have to accept your offer, Mr. Harrison," she managed to say finally. "Wheel House will certainly compensate you for your time—or for any expertise you might have."

Her sarcasm was not lost on him, but it had little effect. He simply smiled that superior smile she already loathed and pushed himself away from the doorframe. "You might as well call me Mark," he said, with a wicked glint in his eye. "Since I seem to be involved in your affairs tonight, whether I want to be or not."

Christine winced inwardly. It had been an unfortunate choice of words, but he couldn't really be blamed for that. But then, to her horror, she flushed, and she knew he was looking at her curiously. Stiffly, glancing away, she said, "Mrs. Mallory, if you could show Mr. Harrison where the water heater is—"

"Yes, of course," the housekeeper said quickly. Gesturing to Harrison, she went hastily out of the office, indicating that he should follow her. Mark Harrison hesitated long enough to stare at Christine, who dredged up enough composure to return his look coolly. He gazed at her for a long minute, and then, wordlessly, he went from the room.

The instant the door closed behind him, Christine sank into Anya's desk chair. Ignoring the crashing slide of the magazines piled there as they slithered to the floor at her feet, Christine glared at the door and thought how much she despised Mark Harrison. He had really enjoyed her discomfort, she realized angrily; he had actually been amused by her plight. He was the rudest man she had ever met, the most insensitive, the most heartless . . . and the most compelling.

Shifting uncomfortably on the chair as that last thought occurred to her, Christine wondered why she had thought such a ridiculous thing. She didn't like Mark Harrison; she hadn't liked him from the moment he had stepped out of his car and treated her like a backward and inept little girl. She liked him less now, for he had made her feel a total incompetent, unable to handle the smallest emergency. He had also made her feel . . . totally female. There had been a certain look in his eyes just now—an expression quickly hidden but just glimpsed, and despite herself, she had responded.

No, no! What was she thinking? Was she out of her mind? She shook her head impatiently, trying to stop the ridiculous thoughts chasing themselves through her mind. Mark Harrison didn't attract her—not in the least. She didn't like dark men, and she certainly didn't like men who thought themselves so superior.

Then why did he make her so nervous?

Nervous? She tried to laugh at the idea. What was the matter with her tonight, anyway? She was never nervous with men; she had always been too sure of herself for that.

Then why wasn't she sure of herself with Mark Harrison?

It was just that he repelled her with that mocking smile and that condescending attitude. He was exactly the kind of man she had always despised: the sort who was accustomed to getting his own way with women; the type who used them and threw them away callously; too confident, too cocky, too selfish ever to get involved himself.

No; she didn't like him; she would never like him; it was an effort even to be civil to him. She hoped that he didn't plan to stay at the inn for long, for while he was here she would be uncomfortable.

And not because he was attractive, either, she told herself resentfully, jumping up from the chair again in an effort to distract herself. She searched furiously through the desk, trying to find Anya's notes. Mark Harrison could be the most handsome, the most sought-after man on earth, and she wouldn't give him a second glance. She was through with men. Well, at least for a while, anyway. She had enough problems right now; she certainly didn't need any more complications in her life at this point.

There was a banging, clanging sound through the house and along the baseboards, and Christine paused. The noise became a series of thumps, and from somewhere in the depths of the inn she heard a soft humming that could only mean the water heater was working again.

"I don't believe it!" she exclaimed aloud, sinking down onto the edge of the desk, a sheaf of Anya's papers in her hand. "He really did fix the stupid thing!"

"Did you think I couldn't?" drawled a voice from the doorway.

Christine whirled around guiltily. The papers

she had in her hand slipped to the floor, and she bent quickly to retrieve them, trying to hide her embarrassment. Then she became angry.

"Do you always sneak up on people like that?" she demanded.

She hadn't realized it, but he had come to help her. They were both squatting on the floor, and their heads were level when she looked up accusingly. Distracted, she saw that his eyes weren't brown, as she had thought, but so deep a color that they were nearly black. He was gazing at her with such a strange expression that she caught her breath. She stared at him, mesmerized by his eyes, drawn toward him despite herself. It was almost as if he had somehow reached out and touched her.

Then she saw amusement leap into his eyes, and she stiffened. He was laughing at her. Laughing! She straightened abruptly, grabbing the last of the papers from the floor, snatching the ones he held from his hand. She was careful not to touch him, but she didn't know why.

"I suppose you think it's funny that I had to ask for your help a second time tonight," she said. To her horror, her voice shook. She looked down at her hands: they were trembling, too. What was the matter with her? Turning quickly away from him, she slammed the papers down on the desk. She felt like a fool. It was all she could do to make herself face him again; she was sure he would see something in her face.

"I'm sorry," she said, striving for composure. "I shouldn't have said that. I do appreciate your help, and I should thank you for it."

Mark seemed about to say something, changed his mind, and paused. Finally he shrugged. "Anytime," he said indifferently. He started to leave, stopped at the door again to look back at her. "Anything else you want me to fix?"

Christine took refuge in anger again. She wished he would stop staring at her that way; it was unnerving. "No, thanks," she said evenly. "You've done enough already."

He closed the door behind him with another shrug, and Christine collapsed against the edge of the desk again. Had she imagined that look in his eyes? Had she wanted it to be there?

No—no! What was wrong with her tonight? Mark Harrison was a rude, impossible man, and she disliked him intensely. He had helped her out only because it amused him. It was as simple as that. He had been laughing at her the whole time, aware of the effect he had on her, and she had been fool enough to let him see it.

What *was* it about him that attracted and repelled her at the same time? She wasn't usually so transparent; in fact, she was just the opposite. She had always been able to hold her own with a man; if she didn't want him to know how she felt, she could dissemble so successfully that she had the reputation of being cold, aloof. It was a reputation she cultivated; it made things so much easier.

Then why had she failed so miserably tonight?

She was just tired, that was all. The long drive, the flat tire, and then being faced with a crisis the instant she arrived had exhausted her. She wasn't thinking clearly—she wasn't thinking at all. She would go to bed, leave everything until morning. Things had to look better then; they could hardly be worse tonight.

And, she thought grimly as she snapped out the office light and went upstairs, tomorrow she would handle herself better with Mark Harrison. He had had her at a disadvantage tonight, but that wasn't going to happen again. She would be prepared the next time she saw him; he wasn't going to catch her off guard a second time. Oh, no, she would make sure of that.

Chapter Two

$\mathcal{A}$nya called early the next morning, full of apologies for not being at the inn when Christine had arrived, but brimming with enthusiasm for the clinic, and relieved to hear that everything was running smoothly at Wheel House. Christine, answering the telephone from Anya's office, and already inundated by invoices, requests for delivery, sample menus for the guests, laundry notes, and a list prepared by Mrs. Mallory, didn't have the heart to dampen Anya's enthusiasm when she asked how things were going.

Suppressing a sigh at the mound of paperwork piled around her, Christine said, "Everything is fine, Anya." She laughed a little. "Confusing, perhaps, but okay. I suppose I'll get it all straightened out eventually."

"I knew you would," Anya said happily.

"Mrs. Mallory has already been a big help. I don't know what I would do without her."

"Me, either!" Anya giggled. "Isn't she exactly what we all pictured in English lit class as the perfect housekeeper?"

Christine agreed. Then she asked carefully, "Anya, who do you call when you need something fixed? I mean, like the plumbing, or things like that."

"Why? Is anything wrong?"

"No, no. Not now, anyway," Christine said hastily. "There was . . . a little difficulty with the water heater last night—"

"Oh, that old thing! I suppose I should have warned you about that. But—I forgot."

Christine raised her eyes heavenward and shook her head, smiling. It would have been a help if Anya had said something about it, but that was typical Anya, she thought. "You've had trouble with it before, I take it," she said dryly.

"Oh, yes," Anya replied airily. "I was going to have it replaced, but so far it's responded to a good, swift kick. Is it all right now?"

"Yes, but I still would like to know who to call—"

"Well, the list of emergency numbers is right there, by the desk!"

Christine glanced around. She had managed to clear away most of the nonessentials—three-year-old magazines, yellowed newspaper clippings, torn recipes—and had piled them all carefully in a box she put behind the door, but she hadn't found a list, and she told Anya so.

"Well, of course I don't keep it *on* the desk!"

Anya said indignantly. "It could get lost! All you have to do is look by the phone, on the wall."

The wall? Christine looked up, and there, scrawled on the wall in Anya's distinctive hand, was a list of phone numbers, names beside them. She didn't know whether to laugh or be irritated at the sight.

"Did you find it?" Anya asked.

"Yes," said Christine wryly. "I found it. Now, if you could just tell me which name to call for what, I'd be eternally grateful."

"The only number you have to know is Elmer's. He's the local handyman, and he can fix anything. I met him in town once, and he told me to call if I ever needed something fixed. He's such a sweet little man, about three years older than God."

Oh, great! Christine thought. But she dutifully placed a check beside Elmer's name.

"Is there anything else?" Anya asked anxiously.

Christine thought of the hundreds of questions she could ask and said instead, "No. I think I can manage. Anya—did you and Peter get settled all right at the clinic?"

"Oh, yes! We met Dr. Shaw last night, and he was very encouraging."

"And Peter? How is he doing?" Christine asked carefully.

Anya was silent for a moment, and then she answered in a subdued voice. "Okay, I think. He's a little nervous, especially about all the counseling they want to do, and I know he's worried about the money. But . . . well, we'll just have to take things as they come, I guess."

"Anya—if you need help, financially—"

"Thanks, Chris," Anya said quickly. "But no. You're doing enough for us already. We'll manage."

"If you're sure—"

"Yes, I'm sure." They were both embarrassed by the mention of money, and now Anya said hastily, "Listen, Chris, I've got to go. We're scheduled for another appointment with Dr. Shaw this morning. I'll keep in touch—and if you need anything, just call."

"The number is somewhere on the wall, right?"

Anya giggled. "You catch on quick, Chris. But then, you always did. Have fun!"

Christine replaced the receiver with a smile. Have fun. She looked at the list of things she had to do and shook her head ruefully. How did Anya, with her scatterbrained ways, ever get it all done? she wondered. Grimacing, she picked up the phone again.

Four hours later, Christine sat back in the chair and rubbed her eyes. Stretching, she looked down at the neatly crossed off items on her list and sighed with satisfaction. She had discussed the menus for the week with Pierre, the French chef; she had approved Mrs. Mallory's choice for a new maid, a girl from nearby Mendocino; she had ordered supplies and sent for laundry. She had answered correspondence and made reservations for two couples who were coming later in the month. Maybe now, she thought, before the next crisis occurred or another list magically appeared, she could go out for a while and take a walk on the beach. She needed to relax, she decided; and she deserved a break now after all her hard work that morning.

Grabbing a heavy sweater, she went out a side door and found a meandering path that led across the grass to the beach. It was September, and the usual morning fog had dissipated, leaving behind a chill breeze, and a sparkling ocean that beckoned. Christine felt the wind lift her hair as soon as she left the shelter of the trees, and she paused at the edge of the cliff, breathing in the crisp, tangy air with pleasure. Far out on the water, she saw a fishing boat bobbing among the whitecaps, and she watched it for a moment, enjoying the sight. A few gulls rode the currents over her head, and down the beach a flock of sandpipers scrambled back and forth as the waves spent themselves on the sand before foaming out to sea again.

There was a series of wooden steps set into the face of the small cliff, and Christine took those down to the beach, thinking how beautiful it was here at Wheel House. As she walked idly along she began to understand what Anya had realized so long before, when she had talked Peter into buying the inn. After the rush and noise of the city, the serenity of the ocean was more effective than any tranquilizer, and now Christine knew why seaside country inns had become so popular. The muted crashing of the waves, the ever-changing pattern of the sea, even the lazy flight of the gulls overhead, were all so relaxing a sight that Christine could feel her own tension slipping away. Problems and distractions that had seemed so important took on a new perspective; seeing the endless vista of ocean and sky diminished worries and concerns, if only for a short time. It was restful, a time to recharge—to approach things in a different light.

Or not to approach them at all, Christine thought, halting abruptly at the sight of another lone figure far down the beach. Squinting against the glare of sun on water, Christine recognized Mark Harrison. She was about to turn away and go back, when she realized that he hadn't seen her. He was standing by the edge of the water, his hands in his pockets, staring out at the sea. He was so still that several gulls had dropped down only a few feet away from him and were unconcernedly basking in the sun.

Christine paused. From this distance, she couldn't see his expression, only his profile and the hard thrust of his jaw. She wanted to retreat before he saw her, but something compelled her to stay, and when he turned suddenly and looked in her direction, it was too late. She stood awkwardly, aware, even from so far away, of the mocking smile he wore as he started walking toward her.

"Hello, Mr. Harrison," she said as he approached. "I hope you're enjoying your stay at Wheel House."

He lifted an eyebrow. "Did you come all the way out here to find out?"

"Of course not," she said sharply. "I was walking on the beach when I saw you. I didn't mean to intrude."

He shrugged. "I have no personal claim on the beach; you're just as free to walk here as I am."

"Well, thank you!"

He had started to walk by her, but he halted again at her sarcasm. "Look, Miss Winters," he said. "I don't mean to be rude, but I came here to be alone. I've got a lot of things on my mind, and—"

Christine was furious. He really did believe that she had followed him out here, she thought incredulously. Was he so egotistic that he thought himself irresistible?

"I've got a few problems of my own, Mr. Harrison," she snapped. "And if you think that I—"

"I don't think anything, Miss Winters," he interrupted with exaggerated patience. "I just know that I want to be alone."

"Well, that's fine with me!" she cried, more incensed by the instant. "But if that's the case, maybe you shouldn't have come to Wheel House. Maybe you should have taken your vacation in a monastery instead!"

"Well, at least then I wouldn't have to worry about fixing flat tires and broken-down old water heaters!"

"I didn't ask you to help! You volunteered, if you remember!"

"And what would you have done if I hadn't?"

"I'd have managed," she shot back.

"Oh? How?"

"I would have found a way. I should have, I see that now. Anything would have been better than having to listen to this! You're the rudest man I've ever met, and you can be sure that *I* won't bother you again. You can be a hermit, for all I care!"

She tossed her head, intending to march away and leave him standing there. She was so furious that she was almost sputtering.

But as she started off he put a hand on her arm, stopping her. "You're right about one thing," he said.

"Oh?" she said icily. "What is that?"

"I have been rude. I apologize."

Without giving her a chance to reply, he turned abruptly and walked away. Christine stared after him, confused and off balance by the sudden change in him. She felt deflated, let down. After all the awful things she had said to him, he had had to apologize, she thought in exasperation. How like him to put her at a disadvantage like that! It wasn't fair.

She watched him walk up the beach, her lips tight. What was it about him that both attracted and repelled her? He had made it clear that he disliked her, and yet she couldn't help wondering why. Was it just feminine vanity that made her wonder? Was she annoyed because he seemed indifferent to her? She realized uncomfortably that her pride was wounded, and she jammed her hands into her pockets angrily.

Mark Harrison didn't mean a thing to her, she assured herself fiercely as she began walking back at a deliberately slow pace so that she wouldn't catch up to him. He could drop dead as far as she was concerned; she didn't need the aggravation he caused, and she certainly didn't want to be subjected to any more of his deliberate rudeness.

Deliberate rudeness? The thought startled her, and she considered it as she climbed the wooden steps toward the inn. It was true, she thought: Mark Harrison was intentionally being as rude as he could be to her.

And for some reason the realization pleased her. She ran all the way back to Wheel House, smiling to herself.

Chapter Three

*C*hristine had made it a point to introduce herself to the guests at Wheel House the night she arrived. Since then, she had been too busy to become familiar with the inn itself, but the morning following her encounter with Mark Harrison on the beach, she decided to have a look around. She soon discovered that while the ocean setting was beautiful, Wheel House had its own charm.

Anya had told her before that the main house had been built in the late 1800s, on a whim of the owner of a big lumber company, as a spectacular guest house for important contacts from the East during their visits to the nearby mill. Two cottages had been added to the property in the 1920s. The cottages, tucked away in a grove of trees, were reached by separate paths, and were cozy and secluded, the perfect place for the honeymooners who were staying there now. But for Christine the original dwelling possessed the most charm.

Anya had given her the largest of the four bedrooms upstairs; it was the only apartment that had its own bathroom. The other three shared the main bath at the end of the hall, but all the rooms had fireplaces, high sloped ceilings, patterned wallpaper, and antique beds of wood and brass. Anya's only concession to modernity was the thick plush carpet that covered the floors, and as Christine glanced into the different rooms, each shining with care and absolutely immaculate, she couldn't help wondering if the carpet covered old-fashioned hardwood floors. It seemed a pity to hide pegged planking, but mornings on the northern California coastline were chilly, even in summertime, and she supposed she couldn't blame Anya for being concerned about the comfort of her guests.

Each of the rooms was decorated in a different color scheme, but all had cheerful patchwork quilts over the beds, and Christine saw by the quality and workmanship that the coverlets were handmade. Inspecting them more closely, she marveled at the thousands of tiny, even stitches in each quilt, at the intricate patterns and varied materials. She would never have the patience to do something like this herself, and her admiration grew for the unknown women who had labored so long to create such lasting beauty.

A vision of herself at work in the agency flashed into Christine's mind as she stood looking at one particularly beautiful piece, and she thought of all the times she had been required to do a layout in fifteen minutes, or write a commercial in an hour—even finish a complete ad campaign overnight. There was nothing of permanence in her work, she realized suddenly: the cleverest commercial was never good enough to last; the wittiest slogan was always replaced by another, newer, catch phrase. A year—even six months—after a hard-fought campaign had been superseded by a succession of fresh ideas, even Christine couldn't easily recall the original concept she had worked so hard to create. There were always other projects, other approaches, different methods, to promote a package or a product. And yet the quilt she was looking at now, crafted by some anonymous woman fifty, even a hundred, years before, endured.

Thoughtfully, Christine went downstairs.

Her vague disquiet stayed with her during her inspection of the rest of the inn, and as she wandered through the dining room, each table covered with a fine damask tablecloth and flowered centerpiece in a crystal vase, she became even more introspective at the signs of craftsmanship all around her. Anya had deliberately clung to the old-fashioned ambience of Wheel House, refurbishing and refinishing the fine antiques to preserve the elegant surroundings of another era. All was as it had been nearly a hundred years before, or close to it. Only the kitchen, with its chrome and Formica, the double ovens and dual ranges, was modern.

From the dining room Christine passed the sun porch where breakfast was served so the guests could sip their coffee and gaze out at the ocean, and she halted there a minute, enjoying as she had the day before the sparkle of sunlight on the sea. Crossing the hall, she went into the living room.

Here the original redwood-paneled walls and ceiling combined to make the large room seem at once cozy and elegant, and Christine paused before the huge old fireplace at one end to admire the intricate carving over the mantel. Anya had told her that every piece of trim in the living room had been hand-shaped and carefully fitted before being rubbed to a fine sheen with hot beeswax to preserve the color and quality of the wood. Once again Christine was reminded of the contrast between today's careless world and the slower, more deliberate work of yesterday. The evidence of care and pride in workmanship was plain to see in the old carvings and polished beams, and Christine's sense of respect increased.

Wondering why she felt suddenly depressed, Christine opened the glass doors at the opposite end of the room and stepped out onto the veranda. The view from this point was breathtaking. She could see across the treetops to the cove where so many ships had come perilously close to running aground during the active days of lumbering in this area. A series of old photographs lining one wall of the living room had given her an idea of the complex and elaborate lumber operations that had existed along the Mendocino coast at the turn of the century, and as she looked out she was amazed to think that men had actually sailed into the dangerous waters here to take on cargo. She shivered, her vivid imagination picturing storms with thrashing seas and foundering ships crashing against the unyielding rocks that lined the cove. Even today, with the weather fine and the wind calm, the waves thundered into the bay, and Christine shivered again.

She was about to return reluctantly to Anya's office and the chores that awaited her there, when she heard a footstep behind her. Startled, she looked around and then smiled at the elderly man who had come out to join her. His name was John Morley, and he and his wife were two of the inn's guests.

"Ah, Miss Winters," he said, returning her greeting. "Enjoying the scenery, are you?"

Christine looked at the panoramic view spread before them. "It's beautiful, isn't it?"

"Yes, it is. My wife and I always look forward to our visit here. It's so restful."

"Do you come often?"

"Every year about this time." The faded blue eyes took on a sparkle. "It's our one luxury, you see."

Christine doubted that; she had seen the Mercedes the Morleys owned. She tried to hide a smile. "I see," she said gravely. "Well, I hope you're enjoying your stay this year, even with the Lyles away."

The sparkle faded. "Oh, yes; we are. It's too bad, though, about Anya and Peter. Such a nice young couple, but so troubled. I hope everything works out for them."

Christine wasn't surprised that John Morley had an inkling of Anya and Peter's problems. It wouldn't be difficult to confide in this kindly old man, and Anya had always been open and outgoing. "I hope so, too," Christine said quietly.

John Morley gestured. "There is another troubled young man, I'm afraid," he said, looking down the path that led to the beach.

Christine followed the direction of Morley's glance and saw Mark Harrison striding along. He walked with his hands in his pockets, his head down, as if deep in thought. As Christine watched him she asked absently, "What do you mean—troubled?"

Morley hesitated, and Christine brought her eyes up to the old man's face. "I'm sorry," she said contritely. "I shouldn't have asked that. It's really none of my business."

"And I shouldn't have said anything," Morley admitted ruefully. "Perhaps I'm just an interfering old man."

Christine gazed into the lined face. "Hardly that, I think."

Morley patted her arm. "Thank you for that, my dear." He smiled. "He did say one thing that I might pass on—to you, since the Lyles aren't here."

"What is that?"

He looked away from her and glanced up at the solid bulk of the house behind them. "He mentioned that the water heater isn't the only problem he found in the basement. It seems that there might be dry rot, as well. And termites."

Christine felt a flash of annoyance. What did Mark Harrison know of termites and dry rot? she wondered irritably. He might have fixed the water heater, but that didn't make him an expert on everything else, as well.

Swallowing her irritation, Christine said, "Thank you for mentioning it to me, Mr. Morley. I'll tell Anya, of course, but I really don't think Mr. Harrison is qualified to—"

Morley smiled gently at her before he turned to go back inside. "Don't be too sure of that, Miss Winters," he said kindly. "Mark Harrison is an architect by profession. I just thought you might like to know."

He had gone before Christine could gather enough composure to thank him. Her face burning with embarrassment at her hasty misjudgment, Christine looked down toward the beach again. The path was empty; Mark Harrison had disappeared behind the trees and she couldn't see him.

It was just as well, she thought with a frown. Even the mention of Mark Harrison seemed to bring out the worst in her, and she didn't know why. She wasn't normally prone to snap judgments—or at least, she amended wryly, she wasn't usually so quick to condemn.

Thoughtfully, Christine tapped her fingers on the wooden balcony railing as she stared in the direction of the beach. Maybe, she thought, she should give the rude Mr. Harrison another chance. She had been taking her meals alone, but tonight perhaps she should come down to dinner. It wouldn't hurt to put in an appearance, to . . . mingle . . . with the guests. Mark Harrison hadn't been averse to a friendly chat with Mr. Morley, it seemed; from that, it appeared that he wasn't quite as aloof as he pretended to be.

Maybe, Christine thought as she left the veranda and walked pensively back to Anya's office for the rest of the day, it was time tonight to assume her neglected duties as hostess.

Christine dressed carefully for dinner that night. She had always had an eye for fashion, and frequently anticipated trends before they became popular—culotte skirts while everyone was wearing pants; slim high heels while others clunked along in chunky wedges. But tonight she tried on and rejected three different outfits before she finally decided what to wear. Annoyed at her indecision and the reason for it, she glared at the discarded clothing on her bed—the black crepe pants and thin gold lace gossamer jacket; the ruffled emerald off-the-shoulder evening dress; a mauve jump suit in tissue faille— before she turned back to her closet in frustration, trying to convince herself that she was only going to so much trouble for Anya's sake. It wasn't true, and she knew it, but she wasn't ready to admit that, of the guests downstairs, there was really only one she wanted to impress.

Impatient with herself and this excessive attention to her appearance, which wasn't like her at all, Christine finally decided on an old favorite. She took a cream-colored silk dress from the hanger and stared at it critically. It had been made for her by an old woman in San Francisco's Chinatown two years before, and the style was timeless in simplicity. Tailored perfectly for

Christine's slender figure, it had a mandarin-style collar and brief capped sleeves, a fitted bodice, and a slim skirt. The only decoration was a thin gold piping—and a wicked slit up the side of the skirt that revealed a long stretch of leg when she walked. Slipping on the dress, she chose a pair of high-heeled sandals in gold, and then stepped back to examine the effect in the mirror.

She had pulled her shoulder-length blond hair back from one ear with a jeweled comb, and she wore the diamond stud earrings her parents had given her for her college graduation. Now she added a heavy hammered gold bracelet to one wrist and leaned forward again. A skillful application of makeup enhanced her green eyes and clear complexion, and with a final touch of lipstick she was ready. The dress emphasized her small waist, trim hips, and long legs, and the total effect, she thought with satisfaction, was very San Francisco: sophisticated, polished, and chic—with just a touch of the exotic to make things interesting.

Pleased with her appearance, and wryly forced to admit to the vanity behind all this slavish attention to detail, Christine went downstairs to dinner.

They were all there when she entered the dining room at the foot of the stairs. Dinner was served at a specified time at Wheel House so Pierre, the chef, could get away at a reasonable hour. The dining room was softly lighted, with flickering candles at each of the tables, illuminating the silver and china and glowing on the faces of the diners. Everyone looked up as Christine paused for an instant in the doorway. Smiling at the young honeymooning couple, Jerry and Janet Simmons, and at the Morleys, who nodded, Christine allowed her glance to roam—casually, she hoped—over the rest of the room.

Mark Harrison was sitting alone at one of the tables by the windows. He had a glass of wine in front of him, and he was smoking a cigarette as he stared beyond the glass to the darkness outside. He hadn't looked up when Christine entered, and at first she was annoyed. Then she laughed scornfully at herself. It served her right, she thought: she had taken all this time and trouble just to impress him, and for all the attention he paid her, she might just as well have dressed in torn jeans and an old sweat shirt. Face it, Christine, she told herself as she went forward to speak briefly to Anya's guests, Mark Harrison just wasn't interested. She had hauled out all her ammunition, and it hadn't had the slightest effect on him. For once in her life, she would have to admit defeat.

The thought was galling.

Unfortunately, now that she had made such a big deal of coming down to speak to the guests, she couldn't avoid Mark Harrison's table without drawing comment. She knew her smile was forced as she walked toward him, and when he glanced—finally—at her, she felt like a fool.

"Mr. Harrison," she said, nodding coolly as she approached.

He lifted his glass. "Miss Winters."

Gritting her teeth, Christine passed by the

table. She went toward the kitchen, as if that had been her intention from the first, and somehow managed to maintain her composure until she pushed open the swinging doors. Pierre, his tall chef's hat askew above his perspiring forehead, looked up in surprise at her entrance. When he saw who it was, his face lit with genuine pleasure.

"Miss Winters! It is an honor to welcome you to my kitchen!" he exclaimed.

"Thank you, Pierre," Christine said, forcing a smile. She gestured. "I just wanted to make sure everything was all right," she added weakly.

"Oh, yes, yes." Pierre had been busily stirring a fragrant sauce. He started to put down the spoon, but Christine motioned with one hand.

"I didn't mean to interrupt," she said quickly. "I was just passing through."

"May I have the pleasure of preparing something special for you?"

She shook her head. "Oh, no—please. I really didn't intend to intrude. Everything smells wonderful, though. Anya is very lucky to have you at Wheel House."

Pierre was a true Frenchman. He brought his thumb and forefinger in a circle to his pursed lips and kissed them. "A lovely lady, Miss Anya! But I am the one who is fortunate!" He glanced proudly around the cluttered kitchen, with its steaming pots and simmering pans, and added, "I have the freedom to create here! It is not like other places I have been, where everything is all hurry and rush, and the food is sacrificed to those who do not appreciate it!" He shook his head sorrowfully and shuddered. "You Americans, with your fondness for hamburgers and ketchup! It is a crime!"

Christine had to laugh. "We're not all gastronomic barbarians, you know!" she protested.

Pierre looked thoughtful. "Yes, that is true," he admitted. "Last night, for instance, one of the guests actually complimented me on the coq en pâté." His eyebrows shot up in remembered surprise as he added, "And he actually knew I had substituted sherry for the Madeira! I think he is really a Frenchman in an American disguise!"

Christine laughed. "You must mean Mr. Morley. He—"

"Oh, no, it was not the older gentleman! It was the other man, Mr.—Harris?"

"Harrison," Christine corrected in surprise.

"Yes. Mr. Harrison. A true gourmet!" He paused, studying Christine, who was still astonished at this revelation about Mark Harrison. "And a handsome gentleman, too, I would say. Is it not so?"

Christine rose from the stool she had perched on. "Only if you like dark, brooding types," she said, smoothing her skirt.

"And Mademoiselle does not?"

"Mademoiselle," Christine said firmly as she went to the other door, "definitely does not."

The kitchen exit led to a flagged walkway around the back of the inn, and from there to a side porch scattered here and there with redwood chairs and tables. Ignoring the furniture, Christine went to the railing and stood there, staring out into the darkness. She could hear the muted crashing of the surf far beyond, and the half-moon was only a dim glow behind a veil of encroaching fog. The air was chill, and Christine had no wrap, but she didn't notice the cold; she was thinking about Mark Harrison, who seemed to make it a point to be pleasant to everyone but her.

What was it about him that intrigued her so? Why did she waste so much time thinking about a man who obviously didn't spare a thought for her?

And what did she know about him, anyway? she asked herself caustically—beyond the fact that he was a rude architect with an appreciation for French cooking?

She had other things to be concerned about, other people to think of. Anya, for instance, and Peter, who were trying to overcome a terrible problem that could ruin their lives and their marriage. She could think about her friend Phyllis, who had married a man twenty years older than she, a man she didn't love, and who had made no secret of that fact—even to her husband, who was very much in love with her, and rich enough to give her everything she wanted. Was Phyllis happy? She had told Christine that she was. Had she any regrets? Christine didn't know. Phyllis never spoke of regrets; she only talked about how fond she was of Harry, who had given her a huge house in the Marin hills, and who took her to Europe at least twice a year.

Then there was her sister, Carla, Christine mused. Carla, who collected men like beads on a string, and who just as quickly discarded a man when a new interest came along. Carla was always in love—or professed to be. She lived a gay, carefree, whirlwind life, devoid of responsibility and filled with fleeting pleasures, always certain that the newest man was *the* man she would love forever. Was she happy? Christine wondered. She didn't see how Carla could be, but then she had never understood her sister at all. They had never been close and probably never would be now. More than a two-year difference in age separated them; it was a lifetime of different goals and values that kept them apart.

And what were her own goals now that she was no longer with McLean and Sullivan? She could easily get a job in a different agency; she could even free-lance if she wanted to. She knew several free-lance copywriters who worked all the time, independently and owing allegiance to no one but themselves. Did she want to be one of them?

What *did* she want? It seemed that everyone else knew her own mind, while she was floundering in a sea of indecision.

Christine had been so preoccupied with her depressing thoughts that it took her a few minutes to realize she wasn't alone. She whirled around and nearly collided with the dark figure of a man standing behind her.

"I didn't mean to startle you," Mark Harrison said smoothly. He was holding two brandy snifters, the liquor gleaming in the faint light like liquid amber. He gestured with one of the glasses. "Join me?"

Christine wanted to refuse. She was determined to refuse. After that casual, indifferent glance he had given her in the dining room, she wanted nothing to do with this man. "Thank you," she said faintly, in spite of herself, as she accepted a brandy and followed him to one of the chairs on the veranda.

She couldn't see his face very well in the darkness, but she knew he was watching her as she seated herself. Nervously, she took a swallow of brandy and nearly choked on it. His silence unnerved her, and she tried to think of something to say. Her mind was a complete blank. What was the matter with her? She had more poise than this.

"Mr. Morley mentioned that you were an architect," she said finally.

"I am."

He was still watching her, but this time Christine was more annoyed than nervous. If he wasn't going to carry on a decent conversation, why had he come out here? She wanted to slam the glass down on the table and stalk away, leaving him sitting here in his own disagreeable company. It would serve him right, she thought angrily. But that was probably what he expected her to do, and she wasn't going to give him the satisfaction of chasing her away. Two could play this game.

"Then you must find Wheel House interesting," she said coolly, sipping her brandy. "Structurally, I mean."

He glanced away from her, toward the dark bulk of the inn, and shrugged. "It has its possibilities. In the right hands, it could be quite a showplace."

Christine rose to the defense. "The Lyles love Wheel House," she said sharply.

Mark looked back at her again. "Loving a house isn't enough," he said flatly. "It has to be cared for, like anything of value."

"I'm aware of that! And so is Anya."

"Anya? Oh, yes, our absentee owner."

"She's not an absentee owner! She lives here all the time with her husband, Peter. The reason that they're not here now—not that it's any of your business—is—" She stopped abruptly. She couldn't tell him the real reason; it seemed disloyal to Anya. "They had to go away," she finished lamely. "On . . . business."

"And so you came to the rescue, is that it?"

"I came to help out, yes."

"Wheel House is a little far gone for help, isn't it?" Mark said lazily, watching her. "It might be better to tear down the whole thing and start over again."

"Tear it down!" She was outraged even at the idea. "You must be out of your mind! This house has stood for almost a hundred years, and with care—" She stopped again, aware that she had nearly fallen into his trap.

It was too late. Mark caught her slip and laughed softly. "That's the key word, isn't it? *Care.* Wheel House hasn't received the proper attention for so long that no one will have to tear it down. It'll fall down by itself."

"No, it won't! Anya won't let that happen— and neither will I!"

"And what about Peter? Does he have a say in this little project, or is he just along for the ride?"

She didn't want to talk about Peter. "Peter has . . . problems," she muttered.

"I see."

He didn't see a thing, and she wanted to tell him so. But she knew that would lead to yet another pointless argument, and it seemed all they did was argue.

"All right, then," she said. "If Wheel House was yours, what would *you* do with it?"

To her surprise, Mark considered for a moment before he answered. Looking at the house again, he said thoughtfully, "It would take a lot of money—"

"Suppose you had the money."

"Well . . ." He put his head back, thinking. "All right. The first thing I'd do would be to go over the entire foundation—replace whatever was needed. Then I'd check the walls, ceilings, attics, roof—the entire roof has to be reshingled, with tiles that have to be custom ordered." He glanced at her. "You're right—they don't make things like they used to; it would have to be a special job. Then, when I was sure that the basic structure was sound again, I'd start refinishing that carved work in the lounge." His voice took on a musing note. "There's some beautiful workmanship there; it should be preserved—"

He stopped abruptly, straightening in the chair, as if he were embarrassed. Swirling the brandy, he took a swallow.

Christine was intrigued by this unexpected side of him, by the reverence that had crept into his voice when he spoke about Wheel House and what he would do to restore it. "Go on," she said softly.

Mark put the brandy snifter down on the table between them. "Go on with what?" he said roughly. He lit a cigarette with a snap of his lighter. "What's the point? I don't own Wheel House. I would *never* own a run-down place like this. It takes too much time and effort. Not to mention money. Houses like this gobble money, and I can't see working that hard just to throw it down the drain."

He stood up suddenly, spinning the cigarette out over the porch rail into the darkness with a flick of his fingers. "You're a romantic, Miss Winters," he said, staring down at her. "And I'm not. The cold reality of it is that places like this should be allowed to die. There's no place for them in this modern, plastic world. They're like dinosaurs, extinct."

Christine leaped to her feet in hot defense. "You're wrong!" she cried. "They shouldn't be allowed to die—they should be preserved. Houses like this are part of history, a reminder of the past—"

"I don't want any reminders of the past," he interrupted harshly. "The past is dead."

There was such violence in his voice that Christine actually shrank back. His eyes, in the faint light from the windows, blazed at her, and his expression was so savage that she nearly cringed away from it. How could he have changed so much? In the space of a few seconds he had become someone she didn't even recognize, and she couldn't think of anything to say.

Mark stared at her a moment longer; then he whipped around without another word and strode back to the house. Still shaken, Christine watched him go. He had scared her with that fierce condemnation of the past, and it wasn't until she heard a distant door slam that she wondered if he hadn't been talking about Wheel House at all, but of something else entirely.

She shivered in the darkness, suddenly cold.

Chapter Four

$\mathscr{P}$hyllis called the next afternoon. Christine, answering the phone from the office where she was going over the endless paperwork concerning the running of the inn, picked up the receiver absently. She had just contacted a local man recommended by Mrs. Mallory to arrange for him to do some gardening work, and she was preoccupied. Her inspection of Wheel House the day before, and her conversation—if she could call it that, she thought—with Mark, had prompted her into action. She had been up early this morning to make another tour of the place, and as confused as she was about him and his criticism of the inn, she had to admit that he had opened her eyes to signs of neglect she hadn't noticed before.

Anya had always been so proud of Wheel House, so enthusiastic about the history of it, so eager to preserve it all. But as Christine had wandered about she saw weeds between the flagstone paths, and bare patches on the lawns. The pond, which she remembered as a charming setting, was murky with algae, and many of the floodlights that were supposed to illuminate the grounds at night were broken.

Thankfully, the interiors of both the main house and the two cottages were immaculate and well cared for; Mrs. Mallory's sharp eyes and supervision of the maids had seen to that. But now that Christine was aware of them, there were too many maintenence problems to ignore.

Was it lack of money? Christine wondered uneasily. Or was it that Anya had been too involved in her difficulties with Peter to notice the decay?

Whichever it was, something would have to be done. Anya had mentioned that business had been slack for the past year, and now that Christine was aware of the neglected air of the inn, she wondered if that was the reason why.

This morning, she had decided to do something about it. If she was responsible for Wheel House while Anya and Peter were away, she could at least put herself to work and improve the place. She had been too introspective, too involved with her own problems and indecision lately. It was time to do what she did best: present the product so that people would buy.

Or, in this case, so that guests would flock to the inn to stay. The ringing of the phone disturbed her thoughts.

"Christine, is that you?"

She recognized the lazy, sultry voice at once. "Phyllis—what a surprise!"

"I thought I'd call to see how things were going. You sounded a little distant when you picked up the phone. Is everything all right?"

"Oh, yes," Christine replied, lying through her teeth. "Everything is fine." She glanced at the clock, saw that it was after eleven, and pictured Phyllis lying luxuriously in bed in her cream and rose bedroom. Teasing, she added, "What are you doing, calling at the crack of dawn? I thought it would be hours yet before you emerged from the satin boudoir!"

Phyllis laughed, a throaty sound that men, especially her husband, Harry, found so sexy. "My dear!" She sniffed, affronted. "I'll have you know that I've already played two sets of tennis, disgusting, sweaty game that it is. Aren't you sorry now that you misjudged me?"

"Very. Forgive me, but I was sure that your chief exercise these days was climbing in and out of your limousine."

"Don't be snide. It's not my fault that rich men find me irresistible. If you weren't so independent, you could have one of your own, instead of slaving away year after year for a pittance and a two-week vacation in Akron."

Christine laughed at that. "It wasn't that bad, and you know it. Besides, I'm not at McLean and Sullivan anymore, remember?"

"Thank God for that. You never met any interesting men there, anyway. And speaking of men, I met one recently that I think you might like."

Christine groaned. Phyllis was an incorrigible

matchmaker. "Who is it now? Another balding banker?"

"Hardly," said Phyllis dryly. "His name is Mark Harrison. He's an architect—or, as he corrected me, a planning engineer. He's going to design a shopping center, or something like that, for Harry. One of those enclosed mall things that are all the rage—wood and glass and plants— sort of like shopping in a petrified forest. Anyway, he— Christine, are you listening to me?"

She wasn't. She had stopped listening the moment she heard the name. It couldn't be, she thought blankly; it couldn't be the same man.

But of course it was, she told herself impatiently. The coincidence was too great. Or perhaps, she wondered suspiciously, it wasn't a coincidence at all. Did Phyllis have something to do with Mark's appearance at the inn? She wouldn't put it past Phyllis to suggest Wheel House to Mark, knowing that Christine was here, too.

"Christine! Are you still there?"

"Yes; I'm here. Describe this Adonis to me."

"Aha! Do I detect a spark of interest?"

"Just tell me what he looks like."

"Well . . ." Phyllis considered. "He's tall and dark, extremely good-looking in a craggy sort of way. And he's very successful; he designed that new medical complex in San Rafael, and he did those gorgeous town houses in the foothills—you know the ones I mean? All aged wood, so that you don't even know they're there. He built the new country club, and . . . oh, a lot of other things."

"He sounds like a real paragon," Christine said lightly, impressed in spite of herself.

"Well, as a matter of fact, he is. He has to be—to put up with that wife of his."

"He's married!" Christine heard the shrill note in her voice and winced. She had never considered the possibility that Mark had a wife. She was so stunned by the news that she blurted, "He's married, and you're trying to set me up with him? Honestly, Phyllis! What a rotten thing to do!"

"Oh, climb down off your high horse," Phyllis drawled. "I should have said his *ex*-wife. A real winner, that one. She had a gorgeous man like that, and she had to run off with some rock singer, for Heaven's sake. A rock singer! Good grief, the little stud is ten years younger than she is, if not more. And, fool that she is, she's filing for divorce. Can you believe it?"

"It doesn't sound too promising, Phyllis," she said evasively. "In fact—"

"Oh, I admit the man is a little battered by it all," Phyllis went on airily. "But that's no problem. You could bring him around in no time if you tried!"

"I'm not sure I want to. He's at the inn now, and—"

"*Is* he?"

"Yes, as if you didn't know! I've already had the dubious pleasure of meeting him, and I can't say I liked it at all."

"Oh, rot! Don't forget, I've met him, too, and I say he's well worth the effort. But listen, Christine, I have to go. The hairdresser, and all that.

Keep in touch, and don't, for God's sake, put on your Ice Queen act!''

Thoughtfully, Christine hung up. She stared at the receiver for a long minute, thinking about the conversation with Phyllis. All right: so now she knew that Mark was an architect, a rude man with an appreciation for French cuisine; that he had been involved in a messy divorce, and that he obviously despised women . . . especially her. Wonderful. If the situation hadn't been exactly promising before, it was positively bleak now.

And why did she care? Why *should* she care? She didn't even like Mark Harrison. It didn't matter to her what his problems were; she had enough of her own.

Frowning, Christine returned to her notes. But despite her determination to forget Mark Harrison, she couldn't concentrate. She kept picturing his face, remembering the arrogant way he held his head, recalling the confident, superior attitude that annoyed her so much. An hour before dinner, she threw down her pen in disgust and decided it was time to take a walk.

The late afternoon held a hint of rain, but Christine didn't care. She had to get out into the fresh air, to stretch her legs and clear her mind, and this time she prepared for the weather. Donning a pair of jeans and a sweater, she pulled on her fleece-lined boots and grabbed a ski jacket before she went outside. Walking with her hands in her pockets and her face lifted to the stiff ocean breeze, she went down the path to the beach.

The rhythmic pounding of the surf was soothing as she walked along, and after a while
Christine began to relax. When she came to a
huge old log that had been washed ashore, she
found a dry place to sit and sank down. It was
almost sunset, and the sun was a glowing
orange ball low on the horizon, tinting the gathering clouds with its last rays, casting a shimmering gold path on the restless sea.

Motionless, Christine sat and watched the
tide, reveling in the play of fading light and color
around her, oblivious to everything but the
ocean and its hypnotic effect. She didn't even
hear him approach. Suddenly he was standing
beside her, and when she did sense his presence
and glance up, the only thing she could think of
was how attractive he was. The disappearing
sun cast a bronze light on his face, so that his
skin seemed to glow. The hard planes of his
cheekbones and jaw were shadowed; his features appeared chiseled, his eyes blacker than
ever. The wind lifted his hair off his forehead,
blowing it back from his face as he stared down
at her with an unreadable expression.

She wished suddenly for a camera. She had
never seen a man look like that, not in the
hundreds of ad pictures with the handsomest of
male models. If she had been able to sculpt, she
thought distractedly, she would have sought a
face like the one she saw now, the embodiment
of . . . man.

"Cigarette?" he said. His voice was husky.
Christine didn't realize what a picture she pre-
sented herself, with her own blond hair blowing
about her face, and the sunset giving her com-

plexion a translucent sheen of gold. Her eyes were enormous, her lips parted in stilled surprise. She was more beautiful than she had been even the night before.

Christine accepted a cigarette from the pack he held out, bemused by the look in his eyes. She rarely smoked, but suddenly she wanted a cigarette badly. She bent forward when he snapped open a lighter, shielding the tiny flame against the wind, and she put out her own hand to guide it to the tip of the cigarette. When their hands touched, it was if they had both received a shock. Christine was shaken by the contact and her response to it, and so, it seemed, was Mark. The flame flickered as she inhaled on the cigarette, but it wasn't solely due to the wind. His hand was trembling, and, noticing, Christine exhaled shakily.

Mark took a cigarette for himself, and then he sat beside her, smoking in silence. Too aware of his presence, Christine looked away. The sun was a semicircle of crimson now, sinking into the ocean, and the evening light bathed them in a mauve-rose glow.

"It's beautiful, isn't it?" she murmured. She was too distracted by him to think coherently.

"Yes. It is."

Mark's voice still held that husky note, and she could sense him staring intently at her. She took another nervous puff from the cigarette.

"Christine . . ."

The sun disappeared abruptly, leaving behind only a shimmering gleam across the water and a last burst of violet in the sky. His face was even more shadowed now when she looked at him, and she couldn't see his expression. It was small comfort to know that he couldn't see hers, either; she had never felt so clumsy, so unsure of herself with a man, so ignorant of what to say.

It was the tension between them, she realized suddenly—a strain that had nothing to do with social awkwardness, but something that sprang from a powerful attraction that she, at least, tried so hard to deny. She didn't know what he was thinking; she only saw that he seemed perfectly in control of himself again, as if his earlier reaction to her had only been a momentary aberration. Or a trick of her own fevered imagination, she thought grimly. Maybe she had only imagined the trembling of his hand because her own had been shaking so badly.

She had to get a grip on herself. She wasn't a naive little girl unaccustomed to male attention; she was a mature woman, and she knew how to handle herself with men. Even this one.

"I talked to a mutual friend of ours today," she said, striving mightily for just the right light touch. She was damned if she was going to let him see how disturbed she was by his mere presence there with her.

He turned those fierce, dark eyes on her again. "Oh? Who?"

"Phyllis Aaron."

"Phyllis?" He was obviously surprised at the name, and Christine suspected the reason why. But she absolutely was not going to reveal Phyllis's matchmaking tendencies, and so she plowed determinedly on.

"Yes; it's a coincidence, isn't it?" she said, forcing herself to sound casual about the conversation. "Phyllis and I went to college together; we've been friends for a long time. She mentioned that you were going to do some kind of project for her husband."

"Yes." Mark sent his spent cigarette spinning into the darkness. Christine followed the tiny glowing arc it made, and then turned in some surprise toward him as he immediately lit another.

So, she thought, he wasn't as detached and indifferent as he pretended. The idea gave her a fierce satisfaction.

"Harry wants me to design an enclosed shopping mall for him," Mark said, drawing heavily on the smoke. "If I do, it will be the fifth one I've done."

"You don't sound very enthusiastic."

Mark leaned forward, forearms on knees, apparently absorbed in the glowing tip of his cigarette. "I'm not."

"It sounds exciting," Christine ventured.

"Not when you build them one after the other."

"You don't have to accept the contracts, you know," Christine said boldly. "You could do something else."

"What? Renovate old houses, places like the inn? There's not much money in that, is there?"

Despite his scorn, Christine thought she detected a note of wistfulness in his voice. "But if you aren't happy building shopping malls, why do you do it?"

"Well I used to have a wife with very expensive tastes. Deborah wanted money, a lot of it, and I was fool enough to work my tail off to get it for her. I didn't know that she wanted something else—something I couldn't give her in a million years."

The rock singer, Christine thought, remembering Phyllis's comment. She wasn't sure what to say.

"I'm sorry," she managed finally.

"Forget it. It's part of the past. Deborah and I never had a good marriage, anyway. We were both too involved—in her."

Christine was almost afraid to ask. "Do you have any children?"

Mark looked at her scornfully. "Children? Are you kidding? Having a child would have ruined Deborah's perfect figure. Not to mention cramping her style. Deborah wasn't the type to haul kids around—she wanted center stage herself."

"I . . . see," Christine said lamely. She didn't know how else to respond. Mark's bitterness was almost a tangible presence; she felt a little overpowered by it.

"Do you?" Mark said, glancing angrily at her and then away again. "I wish to hell I did. All those years—what a waste of time!"

"She must have loved you once—"

Mark laughed, a harsh, ugly sound. "Deborah loved only herself. The pity of it was that I couldn't love her as much as she did."

He stood up suddenly and put out a hand to help her to her feet. He didn't release her hand as she stood, and Christine felt awkward, unsure what to do. He was standing close to her, and when he finally let go of her and put his arms around her instead, it seemed the most natural thing in the world to raise her face to his.

He kissed her lightly at first, and when he sensed her response, he kissed her again. His mouth was hard and demanding, and Christine pressed closer, excited by the contact and wanting more . . . much more. She leaned against him, reveling in the closeness of their bodies, and he held her more tightly. They rocked, caught in an embrace that shook them both.

It was Mark who finally broke away. Breathing heavily, he snatched his mouth from hers and said roughly, "I shouldn't have done that. . . ."

Christine thought at first that he was joking. Amused and breathless herself, she laughed softly. "Why not? We're not children, you know."

"I know."

There was such a note of pain again in his voice that all thought of laughter was banished from her mind. Frowning, she tried to see his expression as he pulled away, but it was too dark. Where was the moonlight when she needed it?

"Mark—"

He let go of her waist and cupped her face with his hands. Dimly, she was aware of the pounding of the surf and the first drops of rain that fell on them, but her whole attention was on Mark and his inexplicable withdrawal. She could feel the faint trembling of his thumb as he moved it across her cheek.

"If only—" he began, and stopped.

"What?"

He dropped his hands. "If only it was a different time . . . another place," he said wrenchingly. "I can't . . . won't . . . Christine," he exploded suddenly, "it just isn't right!"

He started to walk away. Christine raced after him and grabbed his arm, spinning him around to face her.

"You're not going to leave—not like this!" she cried angrily. "You owe me an explanation—at least that!"

She felt his arm tense under her hand, as if he intended to pull free of her grasp. She tightened her grip, too furious and too hurt to let go.

"Look, Christine, you deserve more than I can give—more than I *want* to give. I told myself when Deborah left that I wasn't going to get involved with a woman again, not for a long, long time. It just isn't worth it. And so . . ." He shrugged, trying to appear indifferent.

It was this pose that angered her the most. Furiously, she finished for him, "And so you tested the waters tonight and decided you didn't want to get your feet wet, after all. That was a rotten thing to do, Mark!"

This time it was Christine who left him standing. Spinning on her heel, she marched away, so angry that she was nearly in tears.

Wisely, he let her go. If he had spoken to her again or tried to stop her, she knew she would have said something she might have regretted later. He let her struggle along alone for a few minutes, until her fury spent itself in the effort to walk on the wet sand, and then he caught up to her.

The promised rain had begun in earnest by then, a cold drizzle that stung her face. She hardly noticed it; she had been too aware of him coming up behind her, too tense at the thought that he was going to try to stop her. She was determined to ignore him. She had never felt so humiliated in her life, so . . . so *used*. But if her pride was in shreds, she still had some dignity left, and he was *not* going to reduce her to tears.

"Christine—wait. I want to talk to you."

He was walking beside her now, trying to get her to stop. When he put his hand on her arm, she jerked it away.

"Christine!"

"There isn't any more to say, is there?" she said icily, walking even faster. "I think you made yourself perfectly clear back there."

"No. I didn't. Christine, please stop for a minute and let me explain."

But she didn't want to hear his explanations; he had said more than enough as it was. She just wanted to get as far away from him as fast as possible. Even dignity had a breaking point.

"There isn't any need for explanations," she threw over her shoulder at him. "And there isn't any point in prolonging this dreary scene, as far as I can see."

"Christine—"

"Goodbye, Mark," she said, with finality.

Thankfully, she had reached the wooden steps that led back to the inn. Without hesitating, she started up. When she had reached the top, he was still standing on the beach, and she knew he was staring up at her. She didn't care. Without looking back, she walked swiftly across the grass to the house. It wasn't until she reached the haven of her room that she was crying . . . sobbing.

Slamming the door behind her, she threw herself against it. "Damn him!" she cried to the empty room. *"Damn him!"*

Chapter Five

Christine had regained a little composure by morning. Her face was pale when she looked in the mirror to assess the damage from a restless night and another bout of angry tears after she went to bed, but the slight swelling of her eyelids was taken care of by a cold washcloth and a skillful application of eye shadow. By the time she went downstairs, no one could tell that she had been crying; she knew she looked the way she always did, poised and ready to greet the day.

Inside, she felt rotten.

Mrs. Mallory met her at the foot of the stairs to tell her that the gardener had arrived and was already hard at work and to give her a list of supplies that had to be ordered.

"Oh, yes—and your sister called," Mrs. Mallory concluded. "She said to tell you that she would arrive sometime this morning."

"My sister? Carla?"

Mrs. Mallory looked surprised. "Yes; she said her name was Carla. Why, do you have another sister?"

"No . . . no, I don't. By why is Carla coming here? Did she say?"

"No, I'm afraid not. And of course I didn't ask. I assumed that you knew she was coming."

Christine groaned inwardly as she took the list Mrs. Mallory handed her. Thanking the housekeeper for delivering the message, she forced herself to walk calmly to the office. Once inside, she muttered a curse and stood indecisively, wondering why Carla was coming to Wheel House. Why now, she asked herself angrily, when she least wanted to see her? She had enough problems on her hands; she didn't need her sister and the inevitable clash they engaged in when they got together.

She must want something, Christine decided gloomily as she threw herself into the chair. Carla never showed up unless there had been some crisis in her life, and then she only wanted sympathy—never advice. Then she would go blithely off on the next round of male conquests that ruled her life, and Christine wouldn't see her again until the next catastrophe.

"Oh, damn!" Christine muttered, banging her fist on the desk. She had a few catastrophes to deal with right here, without Carla. She was a little short of sympathy these days, and if her sister thought she could cry on Christine's shoulder before she dashed off again, she had another think coming. Christine didn't have the time or the patience to sort out Carla's problems; she had enough of her own.

Typically, Carla didn't arrive until late afternoon, even though she had promised to be there that morning. By that time, Christine was seething again, so angry at Mark that she thought she was going to explode. They had quarreled again —in the kitchen, of all places, with Pierre as a witness—and hours later, Christine was still furious.

She had gone to the kitchen to have some coffee and to discuss the week's menu with Pierre. She hadn't dreamed that Mark would be there, lounging against one of the counters as if he owned the place, and she had burst through the swinging door in a rush. There was a pencil between her teeth, and she was juggling the menus from Anya's office, her notebook, two cookbooks, and a coffee cup.

"Pierre," she said, trying to talk around the pencil, "if you have time, I'd like to—"

She saw Mark then and stopped so suddenly that the door swung shut behind her, knocking her forward. The notebook flew out of her hand, and she just managed to save the cup by grabbing frantically for it before it hit the floor.

"I must say," Mark drawled in amusement at her ferocious expression, "that you really know how to make an entrance."

Oh, how she despised him! If he wasn't being rude and sarcastic, he was laughing at her. She glared at him again, lifting her chin. Thankfully, she had remembered to take the pencil out of her mouth.

"I was just surprised," she said icily, "to see you in the kitchen. It's not usually a place where Wheel House guests congregate."

"Ah, but the kitchen is the center of the house, isn't it? Pierre and I were just discussing that very fact, weren't we, Pierre?"

Pierre took one look at Christine's face and rushed forward to hand her the fallen notebook. "It was all my fault, Miss Winters," he said. "I thought no harm would be done if Mr. Harrison and I . . . I mean, he was kind enough to suggest . . ."

He trailed off at her expression. So, she thought: Mark wasn't content with criticizing Anya's care of the inn; he felt compelled to consult on the meal planning as well. Did he think she was so incompetent that she couldn't handle things without his help?

The idea infuriated her. What right did he have to interfere? If he was bored here, he could always leave. *She* certainly wouldn't mind. In fact, it would be a relief to have him gone. She had never felt so clumsy and graceless in her life. Every time he saw her, she was either falling on her face or dropping something. What had happened to that poised, sophisticated woman who gave ad presentations to entire board meetings without a qualm? Where was the person who never stammered or fumbled or lost her temper?

What *was* it about this man that made her feel like a gawky teenager with a mouthful of braces and too many arms and legs? And why was *he* so sure of himself all the time? It was maddening. He was maddening, with that superior smile and the challenge in his eyes.

She had to say something; he was laughing at her again. "The kitchen may be the center of the house," she said between her teeth, "but right now . . ."

"Right now," Pierre said, with a ghost of a wink at Mark, "it seems that the kitchen is getting a little too warm. I think I will step outside for some air. You will excuse . . . ?"

He was gone before Christine could protest, and as the door swung shut behind him she glared accusingly at Mark. "Now see what you've done!"

Mark shrugged, grinning. "It wasn't me. You were the one who scared him off."

"*I* scared him off! What does that mean?"

Mark pushed away from the counter. Christine couldn't help herself; as he came toward her she backed up a step. She didn't like that peculiar light in his eyes, and she watched him warily when he paused to glance idly at the menus she had dropped on the table. He leafed through them casually for a moment, and for some reason the gesture didn't seem casual to Christine at all. It seemed a prelude to something else instead, and she tensed when he looked up at her.

"Are you always all business, Miss Winters?" he asked.

What did that mean? She was annoyed and curious at the same time, and for some reason unnerved again by the way he was watching her.

98

"Wheel House is a big responsibility," she said curtly.

"And you take your responsibilities very seriously, don't you?"

She wasn't sure what that meant, either. Was he laughing at her?

"Of course I do!" she snapped. "Don't you?"

He shrugged. "It depends."

"On what?"

"On how important they are."

She wasn't sure where this bizarre conversation was leading; she just knew she didn't want to pursue it. She had had it with Mark Harrison; he had made it crystal clear how he felt about her. And if that mortifying scene on the beach hadn't been enough to convince her, his barbed comments on other occasions had.

She reached for the menus. She would find Pierre and discuss this with him elsewhere, since Mark seemed to have no intention of leaving the kitchen himself. But as her fingers closed around the folders Mark's hand closed around hers.

"We didn't get off to a very good start, did we, Christine?" he said softly.

She was very aware of the warmth of his hand, the way his fingers tightened over hers, imprisoning her so that she couldn't snatch her hand away. But she was even more aware of the look on his face—wistful and demanding at the same time. An odd combination that somehow made her heart beat faster. She felt a warmth spread through her, and knew that her face was flushed with a heat that had nothing to do with the temperature of the kitchen. It was an effort to drag her eyes away from his face—from his eyes. Those dark, fierce eyes that seemed to imprison her more than the pressure of his hand over hers.

She had to get control of herself. In another minute more, he would kiss her, and she would let him, and then God knew what would happen. She was too attracted to him, she thought wildly; she didn't know why, but she was. And she couldn't let this situation get out of hand. He was a dangerous man—a danger to her if she allowed herself to get more involved. He was too bitter, too hurt by his wife. He didn't want Christine; he wanted revenge. And she wasn't going to be the object of a vendetta against women. He could find someone else to take out his frustration on.

"Look, Mr. Harrison," she said, forcing herself to meet his eyes again. She willed her voice under control. If he sensed her weakness, he would take advantage of it. She pulled her hand out from under his and faced him squarely. "I've met men like you before—men who want to play games at the expense of some unsuspecting woman—and I don't like it. I'm not eager to be—"

"Hardly that," he said dryly, watching her with an amused smile.

That smile made her angry. She wanted to be angry; it made things so much . . . safer.

"The point is," she continued icily, "that I'm not interested. You told me the other day that you don't want to get involved. Well, that's fine. I don't either. But neither do I want to engage in some meaningless little affair to gratify your ego."

"Is that what you think I want?"

His eyes had narrowed; his expression was hard as he stared at her. She didn't care; she was really angry now.

"What else?" she snapped. "If you think otherwise, you've certainly hidden it well, haven't you? I told you, I'm just not interested in playing games."

She reached for the menus again, intending to grab them and escape. His hand shot out and gripped her wrist. She struggled, trying to pull away, but his strength was greater than hers, and she was off balance. Before she could prevent herself, she had fallen forward—straight into his arms.

"Ah, Miss Winters," he said, grinning down at her as he held her close. "Was that intentional, or not?"

"Let go of me!" she hissed. She was too aware of the hard length of his body against hers, of the strength and power of his arms. She began struggling again, in a futile effort to free herself. "Let go of me! What if someone comes—"

"Let them," he said, and kissed her.

Christine couldn't help herself; she responded to that kiss with a surge of emotion that shocked her. He held her tightly, and the pressure of his body against hers was exquisite. She wanted to melt into him, to feel not only his arms around her, but his legs entwined with hers, so that they became one. She wanted to feel his hands, those strong hands, touching her, caressing her. She wanted to explore his body, touching him, feeling his skin and the hard muscles underneath. In that instant, she wanted it all: every glorious sensation they could wring from each other.

But not this way. Oh, no; not this way. He was holding her with one arm, so tightly that she couldn't move. He was overpowering her, forcing her to submit to his superior strength, so caught up in his own feelings that he ignored her sound of protest. His tongue probed deeper into her mouth, and one hand was on her breast, caressing her hardened nipple under the fabric of her blouse. He was hurting her.

This wasn't what she wanted at all. She wasn't prepared for some mindless grope in the kitchen, a hurried passionate scene without meaning. It was cheap, tawdry, and degrading.

Anger gave her strength. His fingers were fumbling with the buttons on her blouse when she surprised him by rearing back. She broke away from him, gasping, her hand actually lifted to slap him.

"Oh, dear," someone said. "It seems I came back a little too soon, no? I didn't mean to interrupt—"

Christine whirled around. Pierre was standing there, a silly grin on his face as he looked from her to Mark. She could feel a fiery blush leap up her throat to her face, and Mark looked fierce and bewildered at the same time. The tension between them was almost palpable, and Christine made a tremendous effort to pull herself together. She had never been so mortified in her life.

"You didn't interrupt anything, Pierre," she

said, embarrassment making her voice sharp. She felt hot and disheveled; it was an effort not to glance down to make sure she was dressed.

"Oh," Pierre said uncertainly. "I understand."

Christine wanted to shout that he didn't understand a thing. But she was still off balance herself, still shaken by what had happened between her and Mark. She couldn't look at him; she willed him fiercely to leave.

Mark seemed more in control of himself than she. If he was embarrassed, he didn't show it, for he grinned easily at Pierre and shrugged in one of those man-to-man gestures that immediately infuriated Christine. She wished savagely that she *had* slapped him. Victorian or not, it would have given her immense satisfaction.

"I think it's time for me to leave," Mark said. "Miss Winters seems to feel that I'm intruding here. And that certainly wasn't my intention at all."

Christine knew what he meant this time. His cold expression told her clearly that he regretted their scene as much as she did—if not more. He wasn't disconcerted; he was angry.

Well, that was fine with her. Let him be as angry as he likes, she thought furiously. She returned his cool stare with an icy one of her own, and her eyes followed him coldly as he pushed through the swinging door without a backward glance.

"I'm so sorry, Miss Winters," Pierre said when the door banged shut behind Mark. "I didn't mean—"

"It doesn't matter," Christine said briefly, trying hard to smile. "Now, if we could discuss the menu for the rest of the week, I'll order what you need. . . ."

That had been this morning. By the time Carla arrived in the afternoon, Christine was still seething. Nothing had gone right after that scene in the kitchen, and she was in a foul mood. When she saw her sister whip into the parking lot in front of the inn in a new red MG, pulling into a space clearly marked Reserved, she stood up angrily. How like Carla, she thought in annoyance, to ignore something so plebeian as a parking restriction.

She was still watching from the window when Carla got out of the car and stood there dramatically, tossing her head and smiling wickedly at someone Christine couldn't see. When Mark Harrison sauntered over to the MG, Christine let out her breath in a hiss. She could almost see the avid light in her sister's eye at the appearance of a handsome male, and her own eyes narrowed when Mark reached inside the car to take Carla's suitcase out. The two of them stood there talking, and inside the office Christine began to seethe again.

Lips tight, Christine watched her sister, and it occurred to her, as it had many times before, that there had always been this competition between them, as far back as she could remember. When they were young, they had vied for their parents' attention; as they got older, it had been boys, and then men. Now, if Christine knew her sister, it wouldn't be long before Carla would be scheming to add Mark to her collection of admiring males.

Well, let her have him, Christine thought with a toss of her head. If Mark was attracted to someone like Carla, they deserved each other. She and Carla were as different as night and day.

She had often marveled that they were so opposite, in personality and temperament as well as appearance. Where she was tall and slim and fair, Carla was petite, dark-haired and dark-eyed. Her figure was both rounded and tiny, and she played her small size to the hilt. Carla was adept at acting the helpless fragile female when the occasion warranted it, but Christine knew that her sister was far from delicate, in any way. Carla could take care of herself; she could be ruthless in relationships, oblivious to any feelings but her own, concerned only with herself and what she wanted. She was also shrewd, Christine had to admit, for she had parlayed a divorce from her first husband—a hasty marriage when Carla was only twenty—into a continuing series of alimony checks that allowed her to do exactly as she pleased. She had never worked a day in her twenty-six years, and she had no intention of doing so. She was two years younger than Christine, but Christine felt ages apart from Carla, and centuries older. And as Carla turned with another laughing remark to Mark, Christine wondered glumly why her sister had come to Wheel House, and what she was going to say to her.

"Well, of course, it was all Franz's fault," Carla pouted a few minutes later. She was perched on the edge of the desk so that Christine could receive the full benefit of her sad story. "He was so dreary after I told him I didn't want to see him anymore. I had met this marvelous man at the Waldorf, but Franz just *wouldn't* leave me alone! He kept pestering us, until Jonathan just couldn't stand it! There was a terrible scene, and Jonathan abandoned me, and I was so furious with Franz that I could have killed him! I was so devastated about losing Jonathan that I had to leave New York— and do you know what? Franz followed me! Can you imagine that?"

Christine wasn't sure whether she could or not. Carla had a way of embellishing her stories, and sometimes it was difficult to separate fact from fantasy where her sister was concerned.

"And so, to escape this itinerant ski bum, you decided to repair to Wheel House?" Christine said dryly.

"He wasn't a ski bum!" Carla said indignantly. "He has a good chance for selection on the Olympic team, I'll have you know!"

"He told you that himself, I imagine."

Carla was unaffected by her sister's obvious skepticism. "Of course not," she said with a toss of her head. "His brother did."

"But when this Jonathan came along, you decided that Olympic skiers weren't your style, is that it?"

"Well, of course, there really wasn't a choice, was there? I mean, after all—Jonathan is the head of his own electronics corporation! And Franz was tiresome after a while. All he wanted to do was talk about skiing."

"And when you couldn't get rid of him, you decided to come here."

Carla crossed one small booted foot over the other and reached into her elegant little leather bag for an alligator-skin cigarette case. Lighting a cigarette with a snap from the matching lighter, she shook her head dolefully. "If Franz hadn't ruined it all, I know Jonathan would have proposed. Oh, just think of all those little electronic gadgets going out all over the world—"

"And all the money pouring in," Christine said. "I can see how your heart is broken at the thought of losing such a lucrative proposal."

"I *could* have loved him," Carla said defensively. "You don't know that I didn't!"

"A man you happened to meet in the lobby of a hotel, and only knew for two days?"

"It wasn't just a hotel—it was the *Waldorf!*"

Christine gave up. "How did you know I was here, anyway?"

"Well, I tried your apartment first, of course. But after I called and called, and there was no answer, I telephoned Phyllis to ask where you were. I couldn't believe that you had actually done something so exotic as take a vacation, and naturally I was right."

Carla glanced around for an ashtray and, finding none, finally tapped the cigarette over the wastebasket. "What *is* going on with you, anyway?" she asked curiously. "Phyllis mentioned that you had left the agency. I couldn't believe it! I was sure you were imprisoned there for life, and now I find you running this quaint little inn miles from anywhere." She took a drag and stared with narrowed eyes at Christine through the smoke. "What was it—a man?"

Christine had no intention of dissecting the reasons why she had left McLean and Sullivan —especially with Carla, who would have been hysterical with laughter over the sordid details. She had always believed Christine a prude, and the idea that her sister had quit her job because of a slur against her reputation would have reduced her to helpless hilarity.

"No, it wasn't a man," Christine said with finality.

Fortunately, Carla was easily distracted. "Speaking of men," she said, "what do you think of that gorgeous creature I met outside?"

"Mark Harrison?" Christine said coolly. "He's just one of the guests."

"Just one of the guests!" Carla cried. "You mean you haven't been to bed with him yet?"

"No!"

"What a waste! Honestly, Christine, you really are Victorian!"

Stung, Christine snapped. "He doesn't attract me, that's all. And if you came here to criticize my love life—or lack of it—you can just climb into your little red car and leave now!"

"All right; all right. You don't have to get mad," Carla said in disgust. "I was only teasing. I just thought—"

"Well, don't."

"Okay! I was wrong. You don't have to bite my head off!"

Carla assumed her injured expression, and Christine tried to control her irritation. It was always the same whenever they saw each other, she thought: Carla pushing her to the point of losing her temper, almost as if she took some kind of pleasure in seeing how far she could go. Why did she let her sister get to her like this? Christine wondered dismally. It was ridiculous to be unnerved by such a trivial remark. *Had she been to bed with him yet?* Was she angry with Carla because she had asked—or annoyed with herself because she hadn't?

"Look, Carla," she said, "I've got a lot of things on my mind right now, and I shouldn't have jumped on you. Okay?"

Carla shrugged. "All right. If you say so. But I still think—"

"I know what you think, but let's just leave it at that," Christine interrupted curtly. "I still have some things to take care of before dinner, so could you manage by yourself for a while? We can talk later."

Carla yawned. "I think I'll take a nap. Where can I put my things?"

The last thing Christine wanted was to have her sister room with her. The thought of sharing her suite with Carla was intolerable right now, and so she said hastily, "Take the room next to mine. The second door to the left at the head of the stairs. Fortunately," she added pointedly, "business is slow right now, or we would have had to share a room."

"Don't look so sour, Christine. Someone might think you weren't pleased to see your baby sister, after all."

Grinning at Christine's expression, she left

the office and headed for the stairs and her nap.
Behind her, Christine made a face at the door
and tried to get back to work.

"What do you mean, you haven't been down to
the dining room for dinner?" Carla asked in
disbelief two hours later. "Are you planning to
be a nun, or what?"

Christine shrugged, refusing to rise to the
bait. Carla had rushed into her room demanding
to know what to wear for dinner, and when
Christine had explained that she had either
taken her meals in the small employees' alcove
off the kitchen or had a tray by herself in her
room, Carla had gaped at her in sheer astonishment.

"It just didn't seem right, that's all," Christine
said now, before Carla could renew her attack.
"I didn't want any of the guests to be uncomfortable or think they should invite me to join
them."

"Well, I'm not going to stay up here while
everyone else is enjoying themselves downstairs, like civilized people. Good grief, Christine—what's happened to you? You're acting like
some deranged recluse! Or maybe"—Carla's expression was suddenly sly—"like Joan of Arc,
martyred for the cause. What is going *on*? You
never used to be this way!"

For once, her sister was right, Christine realized uncomfortably. She *hadn't* been herself
lately, and she wasn't sure why. Had that business at the agency put her off balance more than
she knew? Was she using her responsibilities at
the inn as a shield, skulking around out of sight

in some perverse attempt to diminish herself because she felt such a failure?

It wasn't an attractive thought, and Christine was embarrassed by the sting of truth in it. "Give me fifteen minutes to dress," she said decisively, "and I'll meet you downstairs. Dinner is a little dressy here, but don't," she warned, "overdo it."

"Oh, you mean I can't wear my silver brocade gown with the twenty-foot train and my diamond tiara?" Carla teased.

"No—or the Fabergé emeralds, either," Christine answered, smiling.

The two sisters grinned at each other in a rare moment of shared camaraderie, and when Carla dashed out again, Christine gazed after her a little wistfully. She regretted that such moments were so few and far between, and she resolved to make a new effort with her sister.

Christine's resolve lasted all of twenty minutes. She was late joining Carla in the dining room because of an exasperating mascara smear on her collar that necessitated a change of clothes, and when she finally went downstairs, Carla had found someone to keep her company. Annoyed, Christine saw that her sister, instead of taking an empty table, had joined Mark Harrison at his. They were deep in conversation when Christine paused in the doorway, but unfortunately Carla looked up just then and saw her. She gestured, and when Mark turned around to look, Christine knew it was too late to make a quick exit. Seething, she realized she had no choice but to join them.

"I saw poor Mark sitting by himself," Carla said when Christine came up to the table, "and so I asked if we could join him for dinner. He said yes; isn't that nice?"

Christine thought darkly that there hadn't been anything else he could say, not when Carla had so brazenly invited them. She glared at her sister and said, "You shouldn't have asked, Carla. Maybe Mark wanted to be alone."

"Oh, no; he said not. Didn't you, Mark?"

Mark, thus appealed to by the wide-eyed Carla, smoothly disengaged himself from the possessive hand she had put on his arm. He stood to hold a chair for Christine and said lazily, "No man in his right mind would refuse to have dinner with two beautiful women. The pleasure is all mine."

Christine doubted that, but there was no escape. Reluctantly, she seated herself in the chair he pulled out for her, and nodded curtly when he offered her wine from the chilled bottle by the table. Raising her glass in response to some innocuous toast he made, Christine took a sip. She hardly tasted the excellent Pouilly-Fuissé; she was too furious with Carla for putting her in this awkward position, and too angry at Mark for the glint of amusement she had seen in his eye. He was actually enjoying her discomfort, and it was all she could do to meet his gaze with a cool one of her own.

She was so preoccupied with her dark thoughts that it was several seconds before she realized that Carla and Mark had passed from a discussion of what they would have for dinner and were talking about her. Startled, she heard her name and forced her attention back to the table in time to hear Carla laugh.

"Oh, I'm not the clever one in the family," she said modestly. "Christine is. She's always been such a workhorse, while I just flit around, enjoying myself and not doing much of anything."

"Oh, I'm sure that isn't true," Mark said gallantly.

"Oh, but it is!" Carla glanced innocently at Christine, aware that she had managed in one sentence to make her sister seem a dull, humorless grind, while she took on the sheen of a social butterfly. Christine was so angry she couldn't speak, and Carla went demurely on.

"Christine is in advertising, you know," she said, batting her eyes at Mark. She wrinkled her nose in faint distaste. "Such a cutthroat, ruthless business! I never did understand why she chose it."

Mark had been watching Carla's mobile, vivacious face with interest, a smile playing about his lips as she chattered on, obviously flirting with him. This time, though, her plan backfired. At the mention of Christine's profession, he glanced away from Carla and stared curiously at Christine instead.

"Advertising?" he said, lifting an eyebrow. "Somehow, I can't quite picture you in that field."

"Oh, really?" Christine made herself meet his eyes. "Despite what Carla believes, there are some fine, brilliant people in the advertising business. It takes creativity and talent to get to the top, and the challenge can be exhilarating."

Carla wasn't about to allow Christine to become the focus of Mark's attention. "Especially if you don't mind stepping on someone else to get there," she said ingenuously. "I could never do that, myself."

Christine repressed a sharp reply to that blatant falsehood, aware suddenly that Mark was watching them both with interest, alert to the rising tension between her and her sister. She wasn't going to let him think that she and Carla were competing for him, and so she smiled sweetly at Carla and murmured, "No, your talents lie in other areas, don't they?"

Carla affected innocent surprise. "I don't know what you mean, Christine. But anyway, it's all beside the point now, isn't it? You aren't with that stupid agency anymore; you're here, running the inn for Anya." Carla laughed a little and put her hand on Mark's arm again. "Didn't I tell you she was a workhorse? Or perhaps I should say a Florence Nightingale, always rushing to the rescue!"

Christine gritted her teeth. Carla was adept at turning a compliment into a veiled insult, and Christine knew from experience that if she replied sharply to that comment, she would only receive a hurt look from Carla, who would feign surprise that her sister was offended by her seemingly innocent remark. It was a vicious circle, one they had engaged in since childhood, and she wasn't going to play Carla's game tonight.

So now, when she wanted to slap that smug expression from her sister's face, Christine forced herself to say lightly instead, "Florence Nightingale was a nurse, Carla, and I can hardly be considered that—ruthless advertising cut-throat that I am. I think I'll have the poached salmon for dinner. What did you two decide?"

"Since you seem to be the acting hostess here, I'll follow your example," Mark said, pouring more wine. He glanced at her, and Christine was surprised to see a glint of admiration in his eyes before he turned to attend to Carla's empty glass.

Carla was not going to be upstaged a second time. "Oh, how dull!" she exclaimed. "I thought you were going to have the steak tartare, Mark!"

"Not tonight," he said smoothly.

"Well, I am!" Carla said with a toss of her head. "I like my meat red!"

Somehow, Christine managed to get through that meal without braining her sister or losing her temper completely. Carla was in top form that night, displaying all the vivacity that had attracted so many men. Because she was tiny, she could be pixieish and coy without appearing ridiculous, and both Christine and Mark were helpless to stem the constant tide of chatter from Carla, who was enjoying herself thoroughly. Christine had never felt more like the proverbial fifth wheel, and she was both unaccustomed to the feeling and annoyed by it. She was even more annoyed when Mark was interrupted constantly whenever he turned to draw her into the conversation, and as the interminable meal wore on, Christine began to see a change in him. Surrendering to the inevitable, Mark gave up the attempt to initiate conversation and began to be amused by Carla instead.

Christine knew exactly what her sister was doing, and yet she was powerless to prevent it, even if she wanted to. But she was not going to compete with Carla for Mark. He had made it crystal clear how he felt about her, and even if her pride hadn't been wounded over that, she wasn't going to engage in some feminine struggle, with Mark as the prize. She knew that Carla was turning on the charm mainly because she thought Christine was interested in Mark; it was a game her sister had always played, and suddenly Christine was weary of the whole charade.

By the time dessert was served, Christine had developed a fierce headache. She was just seeking an opening in the conversation that would give her an excuse to leave, when Mark turned suddenly toward her.

"You've been very quiet tonight, Christine," he commented as Carla turned to accept dessert from the waitress.

Christine tried to smile casually. Her headache made it difficult for her to think of a clever reply, and so she murmured, "With Carla around, it's hard to get a word in edgewise."

"Yes; I see that."

Christine couldn't tell from his expression whether the remark had been a critical one or not. She doubted it; he seemed to have enjoyed Carla's bright chatter all through the meal.

"Christine—"

But whatever he had been about to say was interrupted by Carla, of course, who demanded that he sample the chocolate truffle cake she had just been served.

"Oh, you have to taste it, at least!" Carla insisted when Mark shook his head.

Christine saw her opening and took it. Rising, she said, "While you two fight over the dessert, I'll excuse myself. It's been a long day, and—"

"Oh, Christine, it's so early!" Carla protested insincerely.

"Yes, but as you pointed out before, I have to work tomorrow."

Mark stood then, with her. "Do you have time for a cappuccino before you leave?"

Christine looked at him. Was he being polite, or did he have another motive?

Whichever it was, Christine didn't want to know. She was tired, annoyed, irritated, and too angry with Carla to want to prolong this evening any further. "No; I'm afraid not," she said evenly. She nodded coolly to Carla, who was watching them avidly between bites of cake. "Carla loves cappuccino," she said. "I know she would be glad to join you. Good night."

Christine walked away then, sensing that Mark was staring after her with that amused expression she hated. She had been too abrupt, she knew, but she couldn't help herself. What was worse, Mark undoubtedly suspected the reason for her sharpness, and was entertained by it. What a fool she had made of herself all evening, letting Carla rattle on, hardly saying a word herself. What was the matter with her?

But she had never been able to act coy and cute, like Carla, Christine thought, climbing into a robe as soon as she reached her room; it just wasn't in her. Instead, in contrast to her sister, she had deliberately cultivated a cool reserve with men, an aloofness that suited her much better.

Or at least it had until tonight, she thought glumly as she threw herself into a chair. Tonight that reserve had backfired; the contrast between her and the vivacious Carla had been too great, and she had felt off balance, uncomfortable. Instead of appearing the cool sophisticate, she realized that she had just seemed haughty and supercilious. It was maddening, this mask she always wore to disguise her true feelings, but she couldn't have taken it off tonight, even if she had tried.

She had wanted to be bright and witty and gay; she had wanted to outshine Carla, to show Mark that there was another side to her. But she hadn't. It had all stuck in her throat, and she had been miserable. Oh, she could turn on the charm in situations where it was meaningless, to be sure: in meetings with agency clients, or in talks with producers or directors—she had done it hundreds of times because it was part of her job. But she had never been able to be superficial when it mattered most.

And it had mattered tonight, she thought depressingly, hating to admit it. Oh, yes; it had mattered, all right. For some perverse reason, she had wanted Mark to notice her, to see her in a new light . . . to realize what he was missing, and to regret the way he had rejected her.

Darn it all, Christine thought angrily. Why did everything have to be so complicated? She had come to Wheel House believing that a change in scene and new responsibilities would give her a fresh perspective. Instead, her life seemed to be in a worse muddle than before. What had happened to all her self-confidence? Where had her hard-won self-assurance disappeared to? She was unsure of herself in a way she had never been before, and she didn't like it.

Christine went to bed that night utterly depressed, frustrated by her seeming inability to control either her life or her feelings, and angrily resolved to put all thought of Mark Harrison out of her mind. He was the one who was responsible for all this emotional disarray, and somehow she had to get a handle on these irrational feelings about him, or she would make a complete fool of herself.

Chapter Six

Anya arrived at noon the next day, in a typical flurry of energy and activity, bursting in unannounced on Christine in the office while she was trying to untangle a delivery error.

"No, no," Christine was saying patiently over the phone to the butcher who had sent a truck that morning, "the order wasn't for five pounds of pork; it was for fifty pounds of pork loin. Fifty. Yes, that's right. I'm sorry, too. No, this afternoon will be fine. Yes. Thank you."

"Well, you seem to have things well in hand!" a voice drawled behind her as Christine hung up the phone with a sigh.

Christine turned, saw Anya in the doorway, and jumped up to hug her. "Anya! What are you doing here? Why didn't you call? Where's Peter? Is he with you? Did everything go well?"

Anya laughed, returning the hug. "One thing

at a time," she protested. "But first, there's someone I want you to meet."

Anya beckoned to the man standing behind her in the hall. "Christine, this is Joel Franklin. Joel, Christine Winters."

They shook hands, murmuring the customary greetings, and Christine noted that his handshake was firm and positive, his fingers warm. She noticed also that his hand held hers a moment longer than was necessary, his eyes meeting hers with a direct interest.

Joel Franklin was of medium height, but he appeared taller than he actually was because he was slim and well built. He was dressed in a tan corduroy blazer and slacks, with an open-necked sport shirt that was not as casual as it looked. To Christine's practiced eye, his clothes were obviously tailored, and he wore them with an assurance that was definitely cosmopolitan. His brown loafers shone, his watch was a thin, expensive gold disk, and there was a gleam of heavy gold chain about his neck. He had dark brown hair, carefully styled, and his face was clean-shaven, with a strong jaw, a straight nose, and a thin mouth. Above his polite smile, his deep-blue eyes were very definitely interested in her.

Aware of that glint of attention in his gaze, Christine felt her confidence return in a rush. She smiled before turning again to Anya, who was watching them with a wicked expression on her own face.

"Why didn't you call?" Christine demanded. "You could at least have let me know you were coming!"

"What? And give you time to hide all the evidence?" Anya teased in return. "No, really, Christine, there wasn't time. Joel found out late last night that he could come today, and so we flew to San Francisco and took a car from there. It was all such a rush that I just forgot to call."

Joel smiled at Christine's confused expression. "It might help if I explained why I'm here," he said. "I'm . . . er . . . one of the editors for *WEST* magazine, and we're doing a layout in a couple of months on country inns—bed and breakfast places, that sort of thing. Since it was my idea, I thought I should get a firsthand look at some of the more popular ones on the Mendocino coast. I figured it would be a good place to start, anyway."

"And so I came to give him the guided tour," Anya chimed in. "What do you think, Chris— isn't it a great idea?"

"Yes, it is," Christine agreed, her fertile imagination already envisioning the benefits Wheel House—and the Lyles—would receive from mention in such a popular magazine. Instantly her thoughts leaped ahead to the layout the magazine might use, the hook that would draw the readers' attention to the article. She had to bring herself up short then, for she was already writing the copy in her mind, creating magical phrases that would sing the praises of the inn. Ruefully she reminded herself that she was no longer in advertising. Writing the article was Joel's job; that was what he was here to do, and she would stay out of it.

"I'm sure Wheel House, with all its history,

will be an interesting subject," she said to Joel. "And after you see all it has to offer, I think you'll agree that it couldn't be in a more beautiful setting."

"From what I've seen so far, I'm already impressed," Joel said with a grin.

Once again Christine felt that surge of self-confidence. Joel Franklin might not have seen much of Wheel House yet, but he was obviously impressed with her, and she felt a glow of very feminine satisfaction at the thought.

"Perhaps we can meet for dinner," she murmured. "While I'm here I'll certainly do what I can to help."

"I was hoping you'd say that," Joel replied, his grin widening.

Behind his back, Anya caught Christine's eye and winked.

"Well, what do you think?" Anya demanded several hours later. She had come up to Christine's room after showing Joel around the inn, chatting knowledgeably about the history of Wheel House while Joel took rapid notes. Now, after he had taken the car for a while to drive to the town of Mendocino to explore there, Anya threw herself into a chair and claimed that she was exhausted.

She didn't look it, thought Christine, observing her friend's animated expression and dancing eyes. But then, Anya had always been adept at disguising the things she didn't want anyone to know.

Anya was not quite as tall as Christine, and

her figure had once been inclined to a slight
plumpness—a rounded appearance that was at
odds with her quick, sharp gestures and brisk
manner. She had lost weight since Christine
had last seen her, and there were faint shadows
under her eyes that hadn't been there before: but
Christine knew it had been a long, exciting day
for Anya, and she put the changes down to that.
Then, too, she knew that Anya must be concerned about Peter and the treatment at the
clinic, so she could be forgiven that slight, gaunt
edge.

But one thing about Anya hadn't changed,
Christine noted with amusement: she still had
that crackling vitality, that air of being in mo-
tion even when she was sitting still, as she was
now. She was always brimming with ideas and
plans for a future that could never arrive quickly
enough for her; at times, she couldn't talk fast
enough to spill forth all the thoughts that
whizzed through her mind. She had naturally
curly dark hair—frizzy, Anya often said with a
laugh—cut into a short style that required mini-
mal care. She had a habit of running her fingers
through it impatiently, making it appear even
more unruly than it already was, and she did so
now, laughing. Anya's eyes were a deep electric
blue, intense and alive, alight with the ever-
changing kaleidoscope of her emotions and
thoughts; her nose was short and tilted, her
mouth mobile and usually curved in a smile.
She had been one of the most popular girls at
school, liked for her ready sense of humor, admired for her sharp intelligence, gently mocked

for her untidiness and air of disorder that even the starchiest of professors had smiled over. Christine had always wondered why, of all the men who had pursued her, Anya had chosen to marry a dark, troubled soul like Peter Lyle, but perhaps her choice wasn't so inexplicable, after all. Anya had so much to give, and Peter, it seemed, needed it all.

"What do I think about what?" Christine asked. "About the magazine article? I think it's a wonderful idea."

"Oh, yes—that. It's a fantastic opportunity for publicity, I agree. And God knows we need it," Anya added fervently. "But what I really meant was—what do you think of Joel?"

"Joel?" Christine echoed cautiously.

"Oh, come on, Chris!" Anya laughed. "You know what I mean!"

Christine grinned. "He's not your usual run of the mill, is he?"

"I guess not! And he isn't wearing a ring, either!"

"I noticed," Christine admitted dryly. "But that doesn't necessarily mean anything. A lot of married men don't, these days."

"Well, I happen to know that he's single, unattached, and unencumbered. What do you think of that?"

"How do you know?"

"I asked him, of course. And he was asking a lot of questions about you today, I might add."

"Oh?"

"Yes—oh," said Anya, not fooled. "He seemed to be quite intrigued by the cool Christine Winters. But was Christine Winters intrigued by the rich, successful, handsome, *interested* Joel Franklin? That is the question!"

Christine laughed. "Good grief, Anya—how should I know? I just met the man!"

"Ah, yes. But one glance is sufficient for a possible yes, an absolute no, or a definite maybe."

"All right, then—how about something between caution and enthusiasm?"

Anya shook her head. "Not good enough. Unless—"

"Unless what?"

"Unless you have someone else in your sights," Anya said slyly. "That Brontë type, for instance—Mark Harrison. Now, *there's* an interesting man!"

"How do you know? You haven't even met him—have you?"

"Well, no. . . . But Phyllis—"

Anya stopped abruptly, her fair complexion turning pink.

"Phyllis what?" asked Christine ominously.

"Oh, I didn't mean to say anything," Anya confessed, her face now a fiery red. "Forget it, will you?"

But Christine's suspicions were aroused. "Don't tell me that Phyllis talked to you about Mark!"

"Oh, is it Mark already? Not Mr. Harrison?"

"Don't try to throw in one of your red herrings! Did Phyllis and you cook up something together about Mark and me? Oh, just wait until I see her! I thought as much, and now I know for sure!"

"Don't be mad, Chris. We just thought—"

"We? So you *were* in on it!"

Anya nodded unhappily. "Oh, look, Chris—I'm sorry. It just seemed like a good idea at the time. Phyllis had met him at Harry's office, and when Harry told her about that messy divorce he was involved in, she . . . well, she called me and asked me if you were coming for sure, and when you would be here."

"Wait a minute! How did Phyllis know I was coming to Wheel House? I didn't tell her until the night I left!"

Anya looked even more unhappy at that. "Well, she . . . she was the one who suggested that I ask you to take over. I didn't want to—I mean, I never would have if you hadn't resigned from the agency, but it seemed that everything worked out so neatly—for everybody. I . . . it seems so silly now, doesn't it, to arrange for you and Mark to be here together. I mean, if anyone can have any man she wants, it's you! You have to beat them all back with a stick!"

"Oh, yes," said Christine dryly. "They just come after me in droves!"

"You aren't mad, are you?"

Anya looked so woebegone that Christine couldn't be angry with her. "No," she said. "But next time—"

"Oh, there won't be a next time!" Anya said earnestly. "From now on, you can find your own men. I won't say another word about anyone. I promise!"

"Including Joel?"

Anya sighed. "You're a hard woman, Christine. All right, then, Joel, too."

"How did you meet him, anyway?"

Anya made a face. "Guess."

"Phyllis at work again—right? Does she have an underground, or what?"

"I guess she just travels in all the right circles."

"Or Harry does."

"Yes. It helps to be filthy rich, doesn't it?"

Christine was about to make a flip reply to that, but something in Anya's tone stopped her. She realized suddenly that Anya had talked about everything that day but the one subject Christine was almost afraid to ask about: Peter.

"Anya . . ."

"What?"

"Anya," Christine said carefully, "you haven't mentioned Peter, or the clinic. Why?"

All the animation left Anya's face. Christine was so alarmed at this that she just stared. Anya seemed in that moment to be so small and vulnerable that Christine wished futilely that she hadn't said anything at all. She had never seen Anya look so . . . defeated. It was as if a mask had been stripped away, revealing a frightened, desperate woman that no one, even Christine, had ever seen.

"Anya?"

"Oh, Chris . . ."

Anya's voice held such a hopeless, helpless note that Christine said hastily, "Look—I shouldn't have asked. If you don't want to talk about it, you don't have to."

Anya looked up, her expression so completely devastated that Christine just prevented herself from rushing over and throwing her arms about her friend in a gesture of comfort. She didn't know what to say.

"It's okay to ask," Anya said in a small voice. "After all, what are friends for?"

And then she burst into tears.

"Oh, Chris," Anya gulped several minutes later between shuddering sobs. "I don't know what to do! The clinic was my last hope . . . I thought it would help Peter, but—"

She broke off again, snatching a handful of tissues from the box Christine had given her. She buried her face, trying hard to get control of herself. Christine looked on helplessly. She had seen Anya cry before—from rare temper or ready sentiment—but she had never seen her cry like this, from sheer desperation. She didn't know what to say to comfort her; she could only put her arms about her friend and hold her tightly as Anya sobbed.

Christine let her cry. Anya had suppressed her tears for so long that when the storm broke, she couldn't stop it. She cried until she was exhausted, and all the while Christine murmured soothing sounds and held her until she couldn't cry anymore. She was drained, empty of tears, when at last she sat up, clutching the empty tissue box.

"Do you want to tell me about it?" Christine asked gently.

Anya nodded. "I feel so stupid, carrying on like this," she said, blowing her nose. "It isn't like me at all."

"Everyone needs a good cry sometimes. Even you."

"I *hate* to cry," Anya muttered.

Christine smiled faintly. She hated it, too.

Anya straightened, wiping her eyes with the back of one hand. "Do you have any cigarettes?"

"You don't smoke!"

"I do now," Anya said grimly. "Never mind; I have some in my purse, wherever it is. Did I bring it in with me?"

Christine glanced around, spied the purse flung haphazardly by the fireplace, and silently handed it across. Anya took out a cigarette, lit it gratefully, and exhaled with a sigh and a grimace.

"Oh, God," she muttered. "How do we get ourselves into these messes?"

"I wish I knew."

Anya's reddened eyes met hers. "You sound as tired of it all as I do."

Christine made a dismissive gesture. She didn't want to talk about her problems, which, in view of Anya's emotional story, seemed minuscule.

"Tell me about Peter," she said quietly.

Anya smiled pensively for a few minutes, gathering her thoughts. Her expression was unguarded, and Christine saw more clearly now the hollows in Anya's cheeks, the shadows under her eyes. Anya had been desperately worried about something for a long, long time.

"I think," Anya said at last, her voice low, "that part of the problem is the way we're all brought up—as girls, I mean. We're all taught to believe that men are so strong, so invulnerable. Oh, not physically; I don't mean that—but emotionally. I think that even the most liberated of us really believe, deep down, that men can handle almost anything. They can get mad, or hurt, or depressed, but something in us women suspects that they have a . . . a core . . . that can't be touched. That no matter what happens, they'll always be strong in themselves because their invulnerability is the source of their strength. I believed it. Didn't you?"

The question was almost plaintive, and Christine was about to agree just to please her when she realized, with a jolt, that she *had* believed it.

"I've never really thought about it that way," she answered slowly, "but yes—I think it's true."

Anya looked wistful. "You know, I really love Peter. I've always loved him, I guess. He was so different from all the men I met in college—so romantic and kind and creative. . . . Do you remember those pictures he used to paint?"

Christine nodded. Before he had put away his brushes, Peter Lyle had been well on his way to becoming a recognized artist. His canvases were great splashes of color that were vibrant and glowing, and yet he could also paint portraits of people, from derelicts to divas, that spoke volumes without saying a word. He had the extraordinary ability to capture, with a line or a single stroke, the essence of a face or an expression, and his paintings had hung in some of the best San Francisco galleries—but not for very long. Anyone seeing those compelling creations was moved to buy, for each one touched a responsive chord in the viewer in some way. Christine owned two of his paintings herself, and she wouldn't have parted with either of them.

And perhaps that was why Anya had married

Peter, Christine thought sadly, and with fresh insight: Peter Lyle could express on canvas the qualities Anya had herself; he could reveal himself in that way, and yet remain hidden at the same time.

But Peter hadn't painted anything in a long, long time, and it was tragic to think that such talent had drowned in a fountain of alcohol.

"Isn't the clinic helping Peter?" Christine asked softly.

Anya looked down at her hands and shook her head.

"But you were so enthusiastic when you called, that day. You said that the doctor was encouraging, and that Peter had responded so well to the program of treatment he outlined."

Anya threw the spent cigarette into the fireplace, her face bitter. "Peter fooled us all, even the doctor. He was . . . sneaking drinks from a flask he brought with him."

"Oh, no!"

"Oh, yes," said Anya grimly. "I don't know where he got the liquor, but I imagine it wasn't difficult for him. He's been hiding bottles for years." Her mouth twisted. "He's become quite adept at it by now."

Christine didn't know what to say. She had never seen Anya so bitter, so lost and hopeless. Wordlessly, she reached out and touched Anya's hand. Anya clung to Christine as if she were a lifeline, squeezing her fingers tightly in an effort not to cry again.

"Was that why you left the clinic?" Christine asked gently.

Anya sighed wearily. "Partly. The doctor thought that . . . that Peter would be better off without me for a few days. He seemed to feel that my presence there was putting pressure on Peter."

"What do you think?"

Anya shook her head. "I don't know. I don't know what to think anymore." She looked at the fire, her expression far away. "I suppose maybe it's true. I wanted Peter to conquer this thing so badly, and I thought that he wanted it, too. But now . . ."

"He agreed to go to the clinic," Christine pointed out quietly. "That must mean he was willing to try."

"Oh, yes—he tried so hard that he was sneaking drinks the first day we were there!"

"It's a tough thing to overcome, Anya. It's an illness, an addiction. Maybe he couldn't help himself."

"If he can't help himself, no one else can!" Anya cried bitterly. "*He* has to want to get well—you know that as well as I do! All the doctors and nurses and clinics in the world can't do a thing for him if he doesn't want to overcome this. It has to be Peter Lyle himself—no one else!"

"You have to understand—"

"Oh, Chris!" Anya cried, tears in her eyes. "I'm so tired of trying to understand—to *be* understanding! I can't take it anymore—I can't!"

"Anya," Christine said desperately, "Peter loves you. You know that."

But Anya wasn't listening to her. Now that she had broken her own silence, she had to tell it all. The words spilled out of her, tinged with acid bitterness and an anger that she could no longer hide.

"You don't know what it's been like these past few years, Chris. You don't know what a changed man Peter is, how awful he can be when he's been drinking. He's mean—Peter, mean! I never thought he could be so cruel. Or abusive. He hit me once—oh, yes; even that. But only once. Because I told him if he ever hit me again, I'd leave him. I meant it, and he knew I did, drunk as he was.

"But that didn't stop him from drinking; oh, no. He just found other ways to be nasty—snide little comments, unfair criticisms. Peter has always been clever with words, and he knows how to say things that hurt the most. Oh, we've been through it all, Chris. Every disgusting cliché you've ever heard about drunks is true. I know; I've been there."

"What are you going to do?" Christine asked when Anya had stopped to take a shuddering breath.

Anya looked up, blinking back tears. "I don't know. I just know that we can't go on like this, Peter and I. It's tearing us apart; killing us . . . me." She made a faint gesture with one hand. "And it's destroying this place, and all we've built here. Look around you, Chris. Do you see all the rooms filled, hear the phone ringing with calls for reservations? Wheel House used to be booked to capacity months in advance, and now we have five guests—five! The staff numbers more than that, and yet I can't let any of them go, because we're pared to the bone already.

"The house and the grounds all need attention, but I can't do everything myself; I don't have the time . . . or the money. And Peter— Peter is no help, drowning himself in booze day and night, not lifting a finger except to raise another glass to his mouth. The only thing he's done for months is drink himself senseless and drive away all the guests because of his disgusting appearance. Would you want to stay here if every time you saw your host he was falling down drunk and totally abusive to you? I wouldn't, and I can't blame anyone else for not wanting to, either. It's a miracle Mrs. Mallory has stayed . . . not to mention Pierre and everyone else! I just don't know what to do!"

Christine knew there was nothing she could say at this point that wouldn't sound meaningless. Aching for her friend, she reached out again instead and grasped Anya's hands.

Anya held on to her tightly, exhausted from her outburst, but relieved by it. Christine knew that Anya had kept everything locked inside her for far too long, trying to hang on through sheer force of will. Even Christine, her best friend, hadn't guessed the depth of the problem, or the heavy responsibilities Anya had borne alone.

But she knew now, and already a plan was forming in her mind. She might not be able to do anything to help Peter overcome his alcoholism, or Anya's despair over it, but she could do something else that would—she hoped—ease the financial strain and put Wheel House back on its feet again. She wouldn't tell Anya about it now; it wasn't the time. She would make all the arrangements first.

Anya stood up exhaustedly. "I have to go lie down for a while," she said. "I can't even think straight anymore." She paused, biting her lip. "I'm sorry I dumped this on you, Chris. I—"

Christine hugged her. "Don't be sorry. You had to tell somebody, or go crazy with it all. I just wish—"

"No; there's nothing you can do. And you helped just by listening. Thanks, Chris—more than I can say."

As Anya picked up her purse and left, Christine was already making a mental list of people she would talk to when the time came. She had been in advertising eight years, she thought with satisfaction, and—as they said on TV—she had a lot of markers she could call in. She intended to use every one of them.

Christine went down to dinner that night with mixed emotions. She felt guilty about keeping her date with Joel Franklin after that emotional scene with Anya, and yet she was excited at the thought of seeing him again. She wouldn't have gone, even so, if Anya hadn't insisted.

"I feel awful," Anya had said when Christine came down to the Lyles' apartment before dinner to see if Anya wanted supper together in her room. "Who said that a crying jag makes you feel better? My eyes are so swollen I can hardly see!"

"Try a cold washcloth," Christine suggested.

"I think I'll have Pierre send me some cucumbers instead. Or is it tea bags? I never remember."

Christine was glad to see that Anya could at least joke a little about her situation; it was a good sign. She said lightly, "Speaking of food and drink, I came to see what you want to do about dinner."

Groaning, Anya threw herself into a chair. "Have you no mercy? I just finished making a complete fool of myself, and now you want me to appear in public—to make scintillating dinner conversation with someone I can't even see?"

"Well, we did promise Joel—"

Anya opened one eye. "No—*you* promised Joel. I never said a word about dinner tonight."

"I know he would understand if we begged off. I can tell him—"

"You won't tell him anything!" Anya bolted upright in the chair, only to fall back with a grimace. "What a headache!" she muttered, holding her head. "Listen, Chris—you go without me, okay? One of us should be there, and the way I feel, it better not be me!"

"Are you sure? Maybe you shouldn't be alone."

"With dark and terrible thoughts, you mean? Oh, go on, Chris. Don't worry about me; I'm fine now . . . honest. Despite that humiliating outburst, I really am a big girl. What I need right now is a long, hot bath, time to think—sensibly, this time—and those cucumbers for my eyes."

"Well, if you're sure . . ." Christine was still doubtful.

"I'm sure!" Anya laughed. "Go on, now; you have only a few minutes to make yourself look absolutely devastating!"

Christine smiled, but as she turned to leave, Anya's face became abruptly serious. "Chris . . ."

"What?"

"I . . . well, I want you to know that I really appreciate all you've done. You've taken over here better than I could have, and I'm more grateful than I can say."

"I'm just glad I could help."

"More than you know, Chris," Anya said solemnly. "And . . . and thanks again for listening. I really needed someone to talk to, I guess, to break down like that. I'm just sorry that it all had to land on you."

Christine smiled, a little shakily. "What are friends for?" she said lightly, and then left, before she started to cry, too.

Joel was waiting for her in the foyer when Christine came downstairs again. His eyes lit with appreciation when he saw her, for Christine was wearing an aquamarine silk dress with a scalloped, embroidered hem that swirled around her slender legs and emphasized her fair complexion and green eyes. She wore her hair up tonight, pulled high on top of her head in a loose knot that allowed a few wispy tendrils to frame her face, and she had added aquamarine eardrops that matched the color of her dress and the high-heeled sandals she wore.

Joel, too, was dressed more formally tonight, in an excellently tailored gray flannel suit with minute wine-colored pinstripes. His tie was Italian silk, his shirt Irish linen, and the watch chain spanning his vest was antique gold. He looked exactly what he was: successful, handsome, and very sure of himself. Christine smiled and held out her hand.

"I thought you forgot our dinner date," he said, tucking her hand—possessively, Christine noticed with an inward smile—under his arm as they headed for the dining room.

"Forget a date with an important guest like you?" she teased. "What kind of article would you write about Wheel House then?"

"Is that all I am—a business appointment who has to be handled with kid gloves for the sake of a magazine article?"

Christine's eyes sparkled as he seated her at a table and then took a chair next to her. "I don't know yet," she said demurely.

"Well, perhaps I'll just have to prove myself."

"That certainly sounds intriguing. In what way?"

"Would it help if I promised to put away any poisoned pens and just act as your escort? Or are you all business?"

"My sister thinks I am."

Joel reached across the table to touch her hand. His eyes never left her face. "And is your sister right?"

Christine turned her hand palm up, lacing her fingers with his. "What do sisters know?" she asked with a wicked smile.

It was the best evening she had had in a long time, Christine thought later, wrapped in a warm robe and sitting by the dying fire alone in her room. Joel had been attentive, interesting, witty, and charming—everything she could have wished for in a date. They had never lacked for conversation, and as they leaped from one subject to another Christine discovered that they had many interests in common, from a love of skiing to a staunch belief in women's rights.

The evening passed far too quickly for both of them, and as they lingered over Amaretto and coffee after dinner in the lounge Christine hoped he wouldn't spoil it all by asking her to go to bed with him. As much as she enjoyed his company, she wasn't ready for that yet, because she had never been one to indulge in casual sex. She didn't believe that a date had to be paid for in some physical way, and while she wasn't a virgin, she had always selected her bed partners with care, interested more in the man himself than a quick, meaningless tumble that more often than not ended a relationship even before it had begun. There was a difference between sex and love, to be sure, and she had never fooled herself into mistaking one for the other. But there was a time for each, and the time had to be right. She thought too much of herself to give herself lightly, as so many did these days, and while she suspected that her ideals were old-fashioned, they had always worked for her.

She was attracted to Joel, as she knew he was to her, and if they eventually did go to bed together, she wanted it to be a decision they had reached spontaneously—not because either of them felt that it was expected of the other.

But Joel didn't ask her to go to bed; instead, he asked her to come to work for *WEST* magazine.

"What?" she said, startled at the abrupt proposal.

Joel smiled at her surprise. "It's not so far afield from what you've been doing in advertising, is it? It's still writing, but from a different perspective. The magazine needs good writers, and you could . . . er . . . write your own ticket. Do whatever you want." He smiled again as he sipped some Amaretto. "Within reason, of course."

"But, Joel," she protested, "you don't even know my qualifications—or if I even have any! And how do you know about my work in advertising?" she added suspiciously.

"Anya told me all about McLean and Sullivan. And what she didn't tell me, I can see for myself," Joel replied smoothly. "You're obviously intelligent, articulate, quick, bright, and imaginative. What else do I need to know?"

Christine laughed, a little self-consciously. "You make me sound like some sort of paragon!"

"Aren't you?"

Christine flushed at the open admiration in his eyes. "I knew I could see the fine hand of Anya Lyle in all of this," she muttered. "And what else did she tell you about me?"

"Only that you resigned from the agency at a time when you had worked your way up to head of your department."

"And did she mention why I had resigned?"

Joel frowned a little. "Yes; she mentioned it. Why? Does it bother you that I know?"

"Only if you think it might be true."

He gave a quick, impatient shake of his head. "Give me a little credit, won't you? Just because I'm a man doesn't mean that I think all women get ahead by lying on their backs."

Christine was embarrassed. "I'm sorry. I suppose I'm still sensitive about what happened. It wasn't . . . very pleasant."

"I imagine not." Joel paused for a moment and then added more briskly, "Well, that's all in the past now, and it's time you looked forward. What do you think about an editorial position at *WEST*?"

Christine had to admit that the offer was tempting. Given carte blanche, she would be free to do what she wanted, and after so many years of deferring to demanding clients and fussy sponsors, it would be refreshing to choose subjects herself. Joel hadn't mentioned salary, but Christine suspected that the financial rewards would be more than generous. Oh, it was tempting, all right . . . and so was the thought of working so closely with Joel.

But there were still other things to consider: leaving San Francisco to move to Los Angeles, for instance; giving up the apartment she loved, and the friends she had cultivated over the past eight years. Then, too, she had so many business contacts in San Francisco, any of whom would give her a job in a minute if she indicated she was available. If she wanted to stay in advertising, it would be foolish to leave the city where she had established herself.

But did she want to stay in advertising? Ah,

yes—as Anya was fond of saying—that was the question.

"I'm afraid I'll have to think about it, Joel," Christine said reluctantly at last. "It's a big decision."

"Oh, and here I thought you would jump at the chance, if only for the opportunity of working with me," he said, grinning.

"Well, I'm sure that will be a factor in my decision," replied Christine with a grin of her own, adding wickedly, "One way or the other."

They laughed together, and as Joel walked her to her room he kissed her lightly, murmuring that he had had a wonderful evening, one he hadn't enjoyed so much in a long time. He kissed her again at the door, his hands resting lightly on either side of her waist, and as the kiss deepened Christine responded. His lips were warm, and she could smell the faint masculine scent of the cologne he wore. It was a kiss of exploration, of defining the measure of their response to each other, rather than one of sheer passion, and they broke away at the same time, smiling at each other in understanding. As Christine looked into his eyes she didn't doubt that he wanted more, but he seemed to sense some hidden reserve in her, something she couldn't explain, even to herself, and he was considerate enough not to press her. She liked him even more for that, and she murmured, "I really enjoyed tonight, Joel. Thank you."

"The pleasure was all mine, I assure you. I hope we can do it again—in fact, why not tomorrow? I found some interesting little places in

Mendocino today, and if you can get away, would you like to have lunch?"

Christine thought of Anya, who would probably insist that she accept the invitation, and she was indecisive. She had abandoned Anya tonight, albeit at Anya's own insistence, but she still felt guilty. She was about to refuse when suddenly she realized that she hadn't seen either Carla or Mark in the dining room tonight. They had gone somewhere together, she was sure, and she was surprised at the stab of jealousy she felt at the thought.

Joel misinterpreted the reason for her slight frown. "I can have you back in two hours," he said.

"Oh, it isn't that—"

"And Anya would probably welcome some time alone," Joel continued innocently. "She mentioned today that you had completely disorganized her office, and she couldn't find a thing."

"Oh, really?" Christine said with mock indignation, still wondering where Mark and Carla were. "Well, in that case, she should definitely have the opportunity to reorganize it all again, so that *I* can't find anything."

"Lunch, then?"

Christine thought of the satisfaction she would feel if Mark saw her with Joel tomorrow. "I'll be ready at twelve," she said with a smile.

Now, after Joel had left her at the door, Christine sat by the fire in her room and thought about the evening with him—and the job offer he had made her. It would be challenging, working in a different field, where she could still utilize her writing talent, she reflected. And it would be exciting, learning new skills and polishing old ones. It would be interesting working with Joel, as well, for he was obviously adept himself, and open to fresh ideas and different outlooks. He was an attractive man in more ways than one, and there had been no constraint between them, as there was between her and . . . Mark.

That last thought surfaced without warning, and Christine was immediately annoyed. She didn't want to think of Mark just now, when she was still buoyed by the pleasant evening with Joel. Mark was an irritation, a thorn in her side, and she tried to channel her thoughts back in their former direction.

It was impossible. Once she had thought about Mark, the inevitable and unwelcome comparison began, and Christine was even more annoyed with herself for not being able to distract herself.

Uncomfortably, she remembered her response to Mark on the beach when he kissed her, and abruptly the embrace with Joel assumed less significance. Kissing Joel had been . . . pleasant. Being kissed by Mark Harrison had been so much more than that. Mark had aroused feelings in her that Joel had barely touched, and Christine was forced to admit that she wouldn't have left Mark at the door tonight as she had Joel; she would have invited him in.

"And where are all your high-minded ideals about sex and love now, Christine?" she muttered to herself, disgusted. Yet she knew, as much as she hated to acknowledge it, that if

Mark had been in Joel's place tonight, she wouldn't have hesitated.

It was a humiliating realization, and Christine got up to stab ferociously at the dying fire, throwing another log on the grate in a shower of sparks that matched her mood.

She was crazy to be attracted to Mark Harrison, she told herself. Absolutely out of her mind. Certifiable. Joel Franklin was everything that Mark was not: charming, attentive, considerate, obviously interested in her, and secure enough not to push her into a relationship she wasn't ready for.

Mark Harrison, on the other hand, didn't have a considerate bone in his body. He was rude, impatient, sullen, and brooding; he demanded more of her than she could give, and yet he withheld everything of himself. He expected everyone—including her—to bow to his wishes, and he . . .

Oh, she could go on and on about his faults, but what was the point? She was a fool, all right. And it was even more humiliating to admit that she couldn't help herself.

Chapter Seven

Christine awoke the next morning with a pounding headache that had nothing to do with the wine she had drunk the night before. As she staggered groggily out of bed for an aspirin, she remembered with a wince that she had stayed up until nearly three, preoccupied with thoughts that had chased away any idea of sleep, until she was simply too exhausted to stay awake.

Now she felt as if she hadn't slept at all, and as she groped her way toward the bathroom her mood was black. She felt thoroughly out of sorts, and as she brushed her teeth savagely she avoided her eyes in the mirror. She wished violently that she had never agreed to come to Wheel House, or that she had never met the two men who seemed to be complicating her life even more than it was before.

After toweling herself dry from a hot shower that didn't improve her mood, Christine jerked a sweater from the drawer and pulled on a pair of jeans. She didn't care what she looked like this morning, she thought darkly, and she stomped downstairs to Anya's office, hoping perversely that no one would see her.

Anya was already there, her own good humor restored, but when she saw Christine's face, she silently handed her a cup of coffee from the hot plate by the desk. "Here," she said calmly. "You look like you need it."

Christine muttered a thank you and threw herself into a chair, ignoring the inevitable slide of papers and magazines that she had disturbed —evidence of Anya's reorganization.

"Want to tell me about it?"

But the sight of Anya's sympathetic expression made Christine ashamed of her black mood. If anyone had a reason to be depressed and ill tempered, it was Anya, who had so many important worries. Beside Anya's real problems, Christine's troubles seemed childish to her, and so she made an effort to seem more cheerful.

"What are you doing up so early?" she asked, gesturing toward the papers on the desk where Anya was working. "I thought I would have a chance to get those taken care of before you came down, but I can see that you're just as much of an early bird as you always were."

Anya laughed. "I wasn't up until all hours last night, remember? I took a hot bath and went to bed right after you left." She studied Christine, her head tilted to one side. "So—how was your date with Joel?"

Christine tried to avoid Anya's sharp eyes. Her friend saw too much at times, and Christine was so unsure of her feelings at this point that she couldn't explain them to herself, much less to Anya.

"Fine," she replied noncommittally.

"*Fine*? Is that all you have to say? You have dinner with a man like Joel Franklin, who is obviously attracted to you, and the only word you can think of is *fine*?"

Christine had to laugh at Anya's indignation. "All right," she admitted, "it was more than that. How *much* more, I'm not ready to say yet."

"Aha! Then you *did* like him!"

"Yes; I liked him. We had a great time." She put down the coffee cup and added casually, "He offered me a job."

"A job! At the magazine? Are you going to take it?"

Christine shrugged. "I don't know that yet, either." She stood up and lifted Anya bodily out of the chair, pushing her toward the door. "Why don't you get out of here and let me get some work done? There's plenty of other things you can do besides messing up my office—like taking a long walk on the beach, for instance. It would do you good."

"But—"

"No buts," said Christine firmly. "Mrs. Mallory and I can take care of everything here, you know. We've got quite a little system going now. She tells me what to do, and I do it."

Anya giggled. "That sounds exactly like the system she and I have! It works pretty well, doesn't it?"

"As a matter of fact, it does. I don't know what I would have done without Mrs. Mallory."

Impulsively, Anya reached out and hugged Christine. "And I don't know what I would have done without you. I don't know how I'll ever repay you, Chris—I mean it."

"You can repay me by taking that walk on the beach. You need some time to yourself before you go back to the clinic." Christine paused, searching Anya's face. "You are going back, aren't you?"

Anya sighed heavily, but she nodded. "Yes; I'm going back. I can't desert Peter now, whether he wants me to or not."

"He doesn't want you to leave him, Anya. He loves you. It's just that he's sick, and he needs time to get well. His going to the clinic in the first place proves that he realizes he can't do it alone. He was willing to ask for help, remember."

"Yes, I know. It's just—oh . . . Enough gloom for one day! I'm going to take that walk, I think. And after that, I'll make reservations to go back to Los Angeles and my errant husband. I think I'll leave tomorrow," she decided, winking at Christine. "That way, you can have Wheel House—and Joel—all to yourself."

Grinning, Anya left the office, and as her quick footsteps faded away Christine sat in her place at the desk and tried to concentrate on the little Anya had left undone. All the staff were diligently performing their separate tasks, the empty rooms were ready for occupancy, the kitchen and laundry orders filled, the new gardener scheduled to come again that afternoon, and Elmer, the handyman, was on his way to see what could be done—economically, Christine hoped—about the new shingles for the roof.

Christine plowed through the list she had made with more determination than eagerness for the job at hand, trying her best to ignore the distracting thoughts that kept interrupting her concentration. When she realized that she had looked out the window for what must be the fifth time in thirty minutes, she sat back in disgust.

What did she care if Mark's black Corvette was gone from the parking lot? she asked herself angrily. What did it matter that she hadn't seen Mark—or Carla—since dinner night before last? She knew her sister was still around—somewhere—because the red MG was still parked conspicuously in the no-parking zone out front, but Carla hadn't been in evidence either since that awful dinner. Were they together, Carla and Mark? Christine tried to tell herself that she didn't care if they were.

But she did.

Twelve o'clock, and her lunch date with Joel seemed forever in coming; but finally they were on their way, driving the few miles up the coast highway to the little town of Mendocino, chatting as easily as they had the night before. Joel took her to a small place he had found, a glassed-in conservatory-style restaurant, scattered with white wrought-iron garden tables and chairs and filled with living plants and flowers that weighted the atmosphere with an almost tropical heaviness, humid and moist. They could hear the muted sound of the sea beyond the windows, a background to the hush of conversation from the few tables that were filled. Christine was relaxed and enjoying herself in Joel's attentive company when she happened to glance toward the entrance to the restaurant. She stiffened. Mark was standing in the doorway, and Carla was beside him, hanging possessively on to his arm.

"Christine, what's the matter? Is something wrong?"

She heard Joel's concerned voice from a long way off. With a fierce effort, she jerked her eyes back to his face and tried to remember what he had asked her.

"Wrong?" she repeated blankly. "No, nothing's wrong. Why do you ask?" She knew she sounded like an idiot, and she made another effort to pull herself together.

"You looked so—so strange for a minute. Are you sure you're all right?"

Christine tried to laugh. "Yes, I'm fine. It's just that I saw my sister come in just now, and I was surprised to see her here."

"Your sister?" Joel turned to look. "Oh, the girl in the red dress? She's with that guest from the inn, I see. Do you want me to invite them to join us?"

"No!" The exclamation burst from her more violently than she intended. Joel looked back at her in surprise, and Christine felt herself flush. She laughed again, a nervous sound that embarrassed her even more. "What I meant," she said, trying to gather a little poise, "was that I prefer to have lunch just with you. Do you mind?"

Joel leaned forward, his eyes alight. "I don't mind at all," he said, reaching impulsively for her hand. "In fact, I hoped you would say that and spare me the necessity of sharing you."

Christine smiled, doing her best to ignore the couple in the doorway, praying that a miracle would occur and they wouldn't notice her. It was a faint hope; Carla's eyes were sharp, and the restaurant was nearly empty. Their table was only partially hidden behind a towering *Ficus*, and she knew that if Carla did spy them here, there would be a scene. Fiercely, she willed them to ignore her and Joel.

Their waitress came just then, and in the business of receiving menus and listening to the girl recite the specials of the day, Christine had time to notice that Mark and Carla were following the hostess to a table at the other end of the room. She was just about to heave an inward sigh of relief, when Mark's glance caught hers. He didn't falter as their eyes made contact, but Christine saw his face tighten in the instant before he looked away. He didn't glance at her again as he seated Carla, and when Christine covertly—and casually—allowed her gaze to wander in that direction a few seconds later, she saw that he was calmly and imperturbably lighting a cigarette as he sat across from her sister.

Dragging her eyes away from him once more, Christine vowed that she wouldn't look that way again. With a determined effort, she began an animated conversation with Joel, hardly aware of what she was saying. She hoped viciously that Mark would see her enjoying herself with such a handsome, attentive man and become insanely jealous.

Fat chance of that, she admitted angrily a few minutes later when their waitress came back to take the order. Despising herself, she glanced across the room again while Joel was speaking to the girl and saw that Mark and Carla were engaged in their own conversation. Or at least, she amended furiously, Carla was talking. Mark was sitting back nonchalantly, his eyes on Carla's face, listening intently. He seemed to be enjoying himself, amused, no doubt, by Carla's wit and charm. What *was* it about her sister that he found so intriguing?

"Christine, you're miles away! Anything you care to let me in on?"

Christine started guiltily. Joel was frankly amused by her preoccupation, but there was a perplexed look in his eyes, as well. "I'm sorry, Joel," she said contritely. "I'm not a very good companion today, am I? I guess I have too many things on my mind."

"It's not surprising," he observed dryly. He cast a carefully neutral glance at the table across the room. "An old flame?"

Christine blushed furiously. Had she been that obvious? "Hardly that!" she said with an embarrassed laugh, trying to regain her poise. "He's just one of the guests at the inn, and a hard-to-please one, at that. We've scarcely said two words to each other since the night he arrived and was so irate about the lack of hot water!"

Launching then into an amusing account of

her first night at Wheel House, Christine tried to distract them both from the subject of Mark Harrison. By the time she had finished, she saw with relief that Joel had been successfully diverted, and for the rest of the meal she made sure that she kept her whole attention focused on her companion. She wasn't going to make a fool of herself again by allowing her thoughts— and her eyes—to wander in the direction of the table in the corner.

Joel ordered chocolate mousse for dessert, but Christine asked for coffee only. She had been so distracted during lunch itself that she hardly remembered tasting the salad and the excellent quiche the waitress had brought, but as she sipped her coffee and watched Joel attack the mousse with relish she regretted her behavior even more. He had exerted himself to be entertaining and interesting, and she had treated him badly by being so preoccupied with Mark. He deserved better than that, Christine admitted guiltily to herself, and on impulse she asked him if he had time for a walk around town before they went back.

"Thought you'd never ask." He grinned and gestured to the waitress for the check.

Christine had hoped they could leave the restaurant without Carla's seeing them, but luck wasn't with her. They were only halfway to the door before she heard her sister call out in surprise to them, and Christine knew that if she ignored her, Carla was perfectly capable of dashing over in person.

Resignedly, Christine looked at Joel and muttered, "I suppose we should go over and speak to them."

Joel grinned at her. "I take it you don't care for your sister."

Christine grimaced. "It would be fair to say that we don't really get along."

"Sibling rivalry?" Joel suggested.

"From the cradle," Christine answered wryly.

Joel was about to say something more, but as they approached, Carla exclaimed loudly, "Christine! Why didn't you come over and have lunch with us?"

"Because Joel and I had already ordered when you came in," Christine replied, avoiding looking at Mark, who had risen.

"Well, you could at least have said hello," Carla pouted. "And introduced us," she added pointedly.

Christine couldn't avoid Mark any longer. She made the introductions quickly, and glanced covertly at him as he and Joel shook hands briefly. Mark's eyes met hers again as Carla said something in acknowledgment to Joel, and Christine was instantly annoyed by the mocking expression she saw on Mark's face.

There wasn't time for her to think of something to say to him, for just then Carla cried, "I know who you are now! You're the editor from that magazine!" She indicated an empty chair, smiling flirtatiously at Joel. "Do sit down and tell us about the article you're going to write!"

"Carla—" Christine began warningly.

But Carla wasn't going to be intimidated. "Oh, come on, Christine! You can't keep such an important man all to yourself! We want to hear all about it, don't we, Mark?"

Christine reflected sourly that Carla seemed to have mended her broken heart more quickly than usual. Her affair with the skier and her defeat in pursuit of the electronics wizard had obviously been consigned to the graveyard of past adventures, and Carla was once again completely herself. She had snared Mark Harrison; now it was clear—to Christine, at least—that she would like to add Joel Franklin to her stable of admirers.

Furious with her sister, and with herself for the stab of jealous envy she felt, Christine decided that as soon as she got her sister alone, she would ask—demand—that she leave Wheel House. Childish or not, Christine wanted her sister gone.

And the competition with her?

The question flashed unbidden into her mind, and Christine writhed inwardly, aware that it was true. Or, at least, part of it was true. She couldn't—wouldn't—compete with her sister, not in Carla's often predatory manner. She thought it was demeaning, this blatant pursuit of male attention, and she wasn't going to imitate Carla in any way. There was something cold and calculating about Carla's approach, and the saddest thing about it was that her sister was never satisfied. She always wanted what she couldn't have; once she had hooked a man, she was no longer interested. It was a game to Carla, and it was often a cruel one.

The conversation had gone on without Christine, and when she forced herself to become attentive again, she heard Mark say, "I read your article about the 'new' architecture in *WEST* last month, Mr. Franklin. I can't say that I agreed with all your conclusions."

Joel seemed amused at Mark's thinly disguised contempt. "I take it you have an interest in architecture, Mr. Harrison?"

"You might say that."

"Mark is an architect himself, Joel," Christine said quickly, aware of rising tension. She glanced in Mark's direction. Was he going to create a scene?

"A planning engineer would be more correct," Mark said. "Although I have designed a few of those skyscrapers Mr. Franklin mentioned with such scorn in his article."

"Oh, I see," Joel replied smoothly. "Then you obviously support the school of steel and glass."

"Yes. I'm one of those designers determined to turn every major city into a towering blank reflection of itself. Or am I misquoting?"

Joel wasn't disturbed by the sarcasm in Mark's tone. "You did read the article, didn't you?" he said, unruffled. "I think I said something to that effect, yes. How flattering to be quoted so exactly."

"One can hardly forget such a harsh judgment, especially when it was based more on opinion than knowledge."

"Joel," Christine said hastily, "I really should be getting back. It's late, and I still have some things to go over with Anya."

Carla had been following the conversation with avid eyes, concerned less with the content than with the underlying friction she sensed between the two men. Now she said, "Oh, Christine! You can't leave now! It was just getting interesting!"

Christine flashed her a murderous glare. The tension she had felt before seemed to have escalated into a civilized duel of words, but she was afraid it would soon become something more. Something . . . ugly. One quick look at Mark's hard expression assured her that he had no intention of trying to smooth things over, and beside her, Joel was trying hard to conceal his annoyance. Christine decided she wasn't going to stand idly by while the two men crossed verbal swords, whether Carla was excited by the prospect or not.

"Joel . . ." she said, touching his arm.

Joel made an obvious attempt to control his irritation. But his smile was strained when he looked at her, and his eyes were angry again when he glanced back at Mark. Nodding to an obviously disappointed Carla, he murmured to her, "Perhaps we can continue this . . . debate . . . at another time. If Mr. Harrison thinks my opinions uninformed, he is more than welcome to try to change my mind."

"Anytime, Mr. Franklin," Mark said coldly. "Anytime."

"I can see why you dislike him," Joel commented as they went out to the car.

"Yes," Christine answered, relieved that they had escaped so easily before the argument had degenerated into a brawl. "I thought you would."

She was furious with Mark for being so rude,

and angry with Carla for encouraging him, but she was determined not to let that tense scene ruin her day.

"Did you really say all those things about modern architecture?" she asked curiously as they drove back to the inn.

Joel laughed. "That, and more, I'm afraid. I was in a particularly foul mood the day I wrote that article, I remember. I had been flying all over the country on business, and it suddenly struck me that everything was beginning to look the same: Dallas, Houston, New York, Chicago —everywhere I looked I was faced with those towering faceless, formless rectangles of glass, crowding in on one another, shutting out the light and the sky. And those modern aberrations called sculpture are even worse!" He shrugged. "I just thought it was time to speak up for a little grace and beauty in our environment, that's all. So that when we look at something, we know what it is; and when we see a skyline, we know what city we're in."

Joel laughed again, a little embarrassed at his vehemence. "End of lecture. I usually don't get so violent about things, but that happens to be a pet peeve of mine."

"So I gathered," Christine said, amused and intrigued by this unforeseen facet of his personality. He was always so composed and controlled that it was refreshing to see him angry for a change, and vocal about it. Until his outburst, she had begun to wonder if he wasn't just a little *too* perfect. Now he seemed more human, and Christine felt her attraction to him growing.

Was their friendly acquaintance destined to

become something more? she wondered, and she was pleased to feel a little thrill of anticipation when he reached across the car seat to grasp her hand. Smiling, she returned the pressure of his fingers. Perhaps, she thought, there was more to Joel than she had believed.

Christine considered the idea again later that afternoon when a huge bouquet of roses was delivered to Wheel House for her. The flowers were from Joel, and the accompanying card read:

Called away on business for a day or two. Couldn't find you to tell you so, and hope these will encourage fond thoughts . . .
                                        Joel

Christine read the card twice before burying her face in the sweet scent of the roses. She smiled then . . . a little wistfully.

Anya came back recharged from her walk on the beach, the shadows gone from her eyes, and a wide grin on her face when she saw the roses.

"I see you've made a conquest!" she cried. "Which one is it? Joel or Mark?"

Christine made a face. "Does Mark really look like the kind of man who would be romantic enough to send two dozen roses?"

"To the right woman, of course!"

"Then I'm not the right woman. Besides, he's much more interested in Carla."

Anya flung herself down on the bed. "Oh, yes, our resident vamp. What is she doing here, anyway? Not that I mind," she added hastily. "I just wondered."

"Well, I mind! She was supposed to be recovering from yet another broken heart, but, as usual, her resilience is amazing."

"I take it, then, that the antidote was Mark Harrison."

"Who seems to be utterly fascinated," Christine said acidly.

Anya tilted her head, studying Christine. "Do I detect a note of jealousy?"

"Are you kidding? Those two are made for each other! I couldn't care less."

"I see."

"What do you mean, 'I see'?"

Anya grinned, amused by Christine's exasperated tone. "Why are you getting mad?" she asked innocently. "I thought you couldn't care less."

"I don't," Christine said curtly. "It's just that I find this conversation a little boring. Do you mind if we talk about something else?"

"Sure." Anya bounced up from the bed again. "I know what you need—a night out. I'm going over to see some friends for dinner tonight, and I want you to come with me. You'll like them, and it will be a nice, relaxed evening. I'm leaving tomorrow, and we can all put our noses back to the grindstone then."

But Christine didn't feel like going out that night. She didn't want company—even Anya's. She wanted to be alone. Begging off despite Anya's pleas, Christine promised to meet her in the morning before she left.

"Are you sure?"

"I'm sure," Christine said firmly, pushing

Anya toward the door. "Remember that long, hot bath and a book in bed? I'm going to follow your example and treat myself to the same thing tonight."

But while she kept part of her promise to Anya and took the bath, Christine didn't go to bed with a good book. She went for a walk on the beach instead, and she was to reflect much later, bitterly, that she should have stayed home and read.

Chapter Eight

$\mathcal{I}$t was a beautiful night for walking. The ever-present wind had died down with the rising of a half-moon, and the sky was clear, dotted with stars. A rare night on the coast, without fog or cloud, with the ocean a soothing, relaxing rumble as Christine strolled along, her hands in the pockets of her fleece jacket. Moonlight illuminated the crests of the waves and silvered the sand, and even though Christine was alone on the beach, she wasn't afraid. She was too preoccupied.

Remembering the roses Joel had sent her had started a chain of questions in her mind, and as she scrunched along in the sand Christine mused that it was time—past time—for her to consider the answers to some of those questions.

Joel hadn't mentioned the job offer again until

he had dropped her off at the office after lunch. They had been standing by the car for a minute before she went in, and Joel had become serious.

"Have you thought about coming to work for the magazine?" he asked, searching her face.

"Yes, I've thought about it," she answered hesitantly.

"And?"

Stalling for time, she said, "Joel, suppose the publisher doesn't think I'm qualified, or—"

Joel laughed. "Oh, he thinks you're qualified, all right!"

"How do you know?"

"Because he's the one who offered you the job."

Christine stared at him. His eyes were sparkling with genuine amusement, and there was a wide smile on his face.

"I don't understand," Christine said, confused. Then she realized what he had said, and she stammered, "You don't mean . . . *you?*"

"Yes—me. I own the magazine, and a few other . . . er . . . businesses as well," Joel said, enjoying her surprise.

"But . . . but . . . Why didn't you *say* something?"

He shrugged. "I didn't want to influence you."

"But you said you were an editor!"

"I am. I just happen to be one with a larger scope than most."

She should have guessed it sooner, she told herself. There were signs of wealth and power that she had ignored, because Joel himself played down those attributes. If she had thought about it at all, she had assumed that he had a private income to supplement his salary.

But she hadn't thought about it, and that was obviously what Joel had intended. She smiled uncertainly at him, a little embarrassed for being so obtuse.

"Christine, I'm not going to press you about the job," Joel told her. "I can see that you need more time to think about it. But I do want you to know that the offer is open for you whenever you want it. We could make a great team, you and I," he continued seriously, his eyes never leaving her face. "And we could travel all over the world if you like."

That was when she knew without doubt that he was offering her more than just a job.

Now, walking alone on the beach, Christine debated about what he had really meant. Was he asking her to become his companion, his mistress—or his wife?

Knowing Joel—or, rather, not really knowing him very well at all, she admitted—she suspected that it might be the last. Why she was so certain of that, she didn't know. Perhaps it was the look she had seen in his eyes, or the tender expression on his face. He wanted her with him, she knew, and he had hinted at that to give her time to think about it. She knew, too, that he would accept any decision she made: if she rejected what might be an offer of marriage, he would agree to another alternative. They would become lovers.

The thought made her pause. Lovers. Husband and wife. Which? Neither?

She didn't know. She liked Joel, was attracted to him. She might even love him . . . one day.

And he had made clear the kind of life he was willing to offer her, wanted to give her. He wasn't the kind of man who was intimidated by a career woman; she could write for the magazine if she desired, or not. She could travel with him, go where she pleased, do what she wished. She could have the very best of both worlds with Joel—freedom, independence, a man who obviously cared for her, everything she could have asked for.

So why did she hesitate? Why wasn't she jumping at the chance?

Disgusted with herself, and frustrated by her inability to make a decision—any decision— Christine kicked at the sand in a fit of pique. The wind chose that moment to rise again, blowing fine grains back into her face and into her eye. Exclaiming at the sting of sand, Christine bent forward, covering her eye with one hand while she searched in her pockets for a tissue with the other.

"Here; take mine."

The voice startled her so badly that she jumped. Eyes streaming, Christine tried to see through tears, but all she could see was a white object flapping at her and the dark shape of a man holding it.

"Do you want some help?" he asked.

"No!" Christine snatched the handkerchief and rubbed her eye. She had recognized his voice at once, even before she saw who it was, and as she scrubbed at her face she wondered darkly why Mark always had her at a disadvantage. It was annoying and unfair, and she wished childishly that he would just disappear.

"What are you doing here?" she muttered ungraciously when she could see again.

He regarded her mockingly. "I thought we had an agreement that we could both walk on the beach if we wished."

She flushed in the darkness. "That wasn't what I meant!"

"What did you mean, then?"

"Did you come out here just to start a fight with me?"

"No. I came out to enjoy the ocean in the moonlight. Why did you come?"

He was baiting her, but she had no intention of rising to it. "To be alone," she snapped, and started to walk away.

He fell into step beside her, but she ignored him. Or tried to. They had had this scene before, she reminded herself angrily; she wasn't going to play it again.

Unfortunately, he had the maddening ability to draw a response from her whether she wanted to give one or not. After a few minutes of silence, he remarked casually, "Has it ever occurred to you that every time we meet we quarrel?"

She barely paused. "There's a reason for that," she said acidly.

"Oh? What?"

He was baiting her again, but this time she didn't care. "The reason," she answered as cuttingly as she could, "is your total lack of consideration for anyone but yourself. You go out of your way to be as awful to everyone as you can."

Except to Carla, she thought furiously, and began walking even faster.

"You mean today, don't you?"

"Today and every other day!" Christine snapped. "But this afternoon with Joel is a perfect example."

"Joel Franklin is an ass."

Christine stopped so abruptly that Mark had taken several more steps before he realized he was walking alone. He halted, too, and turned to look back at her. "What's the matter? Can't you recognize the truth when it's told to you?"

She was so infuriated that she could hardly speak. "That was a terrible thing to say!" she cried. "Just because he criticized your precious buildings—"

"Oh, I see he has converted you. Has he engaged you to be his champion, as well?"

"Joel doesn't need defending," she flung at him.

"Then why are you defending him?"

Christine closed her eyes, so exasperated that she was near tears. She was never going to win an argument with him, she realized, because he knew exactly what to say and how to say it in a way that would infuriate her the most. She took a deep breath, struck suddenly with the hopelessness of it all.

"Look, Mark, we don't seem to be able to carry on a civilized argument, much less a polite conversation. Why don't you just go your way and I'll go mine, and maybe, if we're lucky, we can manage to avoid each other entirely for the rest of your stay at Wheel House."

"Would you really like that?"

She couldn't believe the gall of the man. "Yes," she said, her voice steely. "Just leave me alone. In fact, why don't you go find Carla? You seem to get along very well, the two of you. But then, you're kindred spirits, aren't you?"

She started to whip around, intending to walk away from him, but he reached out and took hold of her shoulders. She could feel the pressure of his fingers even through the fleece of her coat, but something in his face prevented her from struggling to break away.

"I don't want Carla," he said hoarsely. "I want you."

Christine had the hysterical urge to laugh in his face. She thought of a score of derisive remarks to say to that and rejected them all in the space of a heartbeat. Now, when she needed a quick and scathing response, she couldn't think of a thing to say. She could only stand there stupidly, mesmerized by the look on his face.

She had dreamed of this moment, longed for it, pictured it a hundred times in fantasy—how *she* would be the one to reject him; how *she* would be the one to fling his mockery back into his face. Oh, she had planned it all, every step, every word. And now that the time had come for her stellar performance, she was frozen. The only reality was the fast and furious pounding of her heart, a pulsing that was so loud in her ears that she was frantically sure he could hear it, too.

She tried to speak, and couldn't. He seemed about to say something, and couldn't speak, either. They were locked in an electrified silence, capable only of looking at each other, when there was so much to say.

He bent his head toward her, and in the moonlight she could see a pulse throbbing in his temple. His fingers tightened again on her shoulders. She was consumed suddenly with the need for him to kiss her, to hold her . . . to love her. Nothing seemed more important than that —no reason, no logic. No memories of past quarrels or snide remarks or sneering looks. She had never felt this way before with any man; she had never dreamed that she would *want* so deeply that nothing else mattered. She felt as if she were on fire, every nerve exposed, every muscle taut with that powerful, overwhelming desire. She trembled with the sheer rawness of her emotion, and Mark shuddered in response. His breath was warm on her face as he brought his mouth down to hers.

They sank down to the sand, locked in a tight embrace, straining against each other, hungry for more. His hand slid under her jacket, his fingers seeking her bare skin, and she moaned when he found her breast. He came down on top of her, and she put her own hands under his shirt, feeling the broad muscles of his back, holding him fiercely to her. They tore at their clothes then in a frenzy, eager to feel flesh against bare flesh, to bury themselves in each other.

The cold night air was a shock on her skin; Christine felt her nipples contract in response to it, and she shivered. Then Mark's warm body covered hers; and she wasn't cold anymore. She was on fire, every nerve tingling. The cool air, the crashing surf, even the sand beneath her, added to the sensations she felt. It was like a dream, a fantasy that had leaped to life with one touch, and Christine moaned as Mark's lips sought hers. His hands roamed her body, touching, kneading, caressing.

His mouth was hot and demanding, evoking a response from her that made her cry out in pure pleasure. She wound her fingers in his hair, holding him to her, straining against him. Her legs locked around him, imprisoning him, and they rolled from side to side. He buried his head in her shoulder, biting gently at the curve of her neck, and she pushed him down so that his mouth could fasten on her breast.

When he entered her, swiftly and surely, with one powerful thrust, Christine locked her legs around him again, arching up against him so that they were truly one. She was transported. She had never experienced such intense, instant pleasure, such complete and powerful sensation. She rode with it, wave after wave, and didn't even hear the wordless sounds of pleasure that were torn from her throat . . . and from his. They were straining, physical beings locked in the ultimate expression of their bodies—aware, and yet not aware, of each other, driving to prolong the shuddering intensity of the moment.

Gradually the wave receded, leaving them both gasping and spent with the force of their union. Mark moved to her side, pulling her with him so that she was nestled against him, her head on his chest. She could hear the hard pounding of his heart under her ear, and she smiled in the darkness, knowing that it had been as good for him as it had been for her. Sighing, she closed her eyes.

They lay like that for a few minutes, catching their breath, enjoying each other. Then Mark reached around and fumbled in the sand for his jacket. He took two cigarettes from the pocket, lit them, and gave one to her while he inhaled deeply on the other. He spread the jacket over her, and she pressed closer, luxuriating in the warmth and pleasure of his bare skin next to hers.

They smoked in silence, reveling in the perfection of the moment—that wonderful sense of lazy timelessness that comes when the body is satiated and the mind at rest. Christine never wanted that moment to end, but of course it did. Eventually other sensations intruded, and despite the shelter of Mark's jacket and his body warming hers, she began to shiver.

Neither of them had noticed during their frenzied lovemaking, but the breeze that had been so gentle before had stiffened, bringing with it a chilling mist. The fog was rolling in, great puffs that obscured the moon, and suddenly Christine was cold.

Mark felt her shiver against him, and his arm tightened around her, drawing her closer to him. He kissed the top of her head, then murmured reluctantly, "I suppose we should get dressed. I don't want you to catch cold."

Christine wanted to deny that she felt anything but a warm lassitude; she wanted to assure him that she was utterly content just lying here next to him. But the more she tried to control it, the worse she shivered. When her teeth began to chatter, Mark sat up.

"That's it," he said authoritatively. "You're freezing, whether you want to admit it or not." He glanced around, grabbed her discarded clothing, and gave the bundle to her. "I guess we're lucky it didn't blow away," he said with a relaxed grin. "What a picture *that* would have made—the two of us sneaking back to the inn stark naked!"

Christine laughed, but inside she was furious with herself. This never happened in books or movies, she thought blackly as she climbed into her clothes, shaking with cold. Everyone was always oblivious of any discomfort or distress in stories; by now the hero and heroine would be locked once more in passionate embrace, murmuring endearments to each other while they waited for a glorious sunrise. All Christine could think of was how cold she was, and how miserable she felt for ruining such a perfect moment. She couldn't concentrate on sunrises or sunsets or murmured endearments; she could only think how wonderful a hot toddy would taste, and how glorious it would be to sit by a roaring fire while she drank it. Some heroine *she* was.

Mark finished dressing and held out a hand to pull her up. His eyes danced when he saw her wretched expression, and as if he had read her thoughts, he put his arms around her comfortingly. "Not like in the movies, is it?" he asked with a soft laugh.

"Oh, Mark!"

"Shhh. It's all right. I never did like those

brassy heroines, anyway. How about a hot toddy? Or maybe," he added wickedly, "you would prefer a cup of cocoa."

She pushed him away, laughing, delighted at the change in him, and a little amazed by it. He caught her, kissed her playfully, and then grabbed her hand. Pulling her with him, he began running up the beach, and by the time they had reached the inn, they were breathless, helpless with laughter, and dizzy from the long run in the sand. They ran straight into disaster.

To Christine's utter astonishment, Peter Lyle was in the foyer when she and Mark tumbled in. The humorous remark she had been about to make died on her lips when she saw Peter there, and she stared, appalled, when he turned to look blearily at them.

"Peter!" she said, and then stopped. She couldn't believe it. Not only was he here, instead of at the clinic in Los Angeles where she had thought him to be, but, even worse, he had been drinking . . . hard.

Chapter Nine

Christine hadn't seen Peter for a long time, but even so, she was completely taken aback by the change in him. He had always been a slight man, slenderly built, but now he appeared gaunt, almost emaciated. He was wearing a corduroy jacket and jeans, and the garments literally hung on him. Bony wrists protruded from his cuffs, and his hands and face were nearly skeletal. He was pale, ill looking, and his blond hair was limp against his narrow skull. He looked like a caricature of himself; the only color in his face was his eyes, which were red-rimmed and bloodshot. He hadn't shaved, and the stubble of beard added to his disheveled, nearly derelict appearance. His hands were never still.

"Peter!" she managed to say again, still

shocked by the sight. "What are you doing here?"

Peter's reddened eyes went from her to Mark, then back to Christine again. "I live here," he said nastily.

"But . . . but you're supposed to be at the clinic!"

Peter uttered an obscenity, and beside her, Mark stiffened. "Better watch your language, buddy," he said evenly.

"And who are you?" Peter snarled.

Mark started forward, but Christine put a hasty hand out, holding him back. She had never seen Peter like this, and she was frightened. Was he just drunk—or had he taken drugs, too?

"Peter," she said cautiously, "why don't we go into your living room, and—"

"What's the matter, Christine? Are you afraid that some of the paying customers will see their host in such a disgusting condition?"

Christine was afraid of just that. "No, of course not," she answered soothingly. "I just thought—"

"I don't give a damn what you thought!" Peter shouted suddenly. He waved his hands in the air, throwing his head back to shout even louder, "I don't give a damn what anyone thinks!"

Mark's voice cut across the space between them like a knife. "I told you once to watch your language, mister; I'm not going to tell you again."

Peter lowered his head, like a bull about to charge. "You're not going to tell me anything,

Mr. whoever-you-are," he snarled. To Christine's horror, he actually sprang at Mark with closed fists.

"Mark!" she cried.

But Peter was no match for Mark, even if he had been sober enough to keep his balance. He staggered, crashing into the taller, heavier man, and Mark held him easily, nearly supporting him entirely as Peter's head lolled drunkenly on his shoulders.

"Peter, what are you doing?" Christine cried, appalled.

But Peter was beyond answering. He slumped down so suddenly that even Mark staggered under the deadweight. "He can't hear you," he said grimly to Christine. "He passed out."

"Thank God! Do you think we can get him into Anya's apartment?"

Mark nodded, his expression as disgusted as Christine herself felt. Silently, he bent over and lifted the unconscious Peter. He heaved him unceremoniously over his shoulder and gestured for Christine to lead the way.

In the Lyle apartment, with Peter safely deposited on the couch, Christine met Mark's eyes and grimaced. She reflected sourly that Peter's little display had effectively spoiled the entire evening, destroying the closeness she had shared too briefly with Mark. What had taken place on the beach seemed far away, dreamlike, almost as if it had never happened.

"Where's Anya?" Mark asked with a frown. He sensed Christine's worry, and begrudged it. He looked at Peter with disgust again, knowing that his appearance had changed her in some way.

"She went out to dinner with some friends. I don't know where," Christine answered distractedly. She hadn't thought to ask the number, and she cursed the omission. But how could she have foreseen Peter's unexpected presence at the inn, when he should have been safely tucked away in Los Angeles? She looked at Peter, too. Did his arrival mean that he had abandoned the clinic, and the treatment? It was an awful thought, and she wondered how Anya was going to react to that. She felt a sharp anger at Peter for doing this to Anya, and only just prevented herself from trying to shake him out of his stupor. What was the matter with him? she wondered impatiently. If he didn't give a care about himself, he could at least have spared a thought for his wife, who was trying so hard to help him.

Then Christine was ashamed of her anger. Hadn't she been the one to tell Anya that Peter was sick; that alcoholism was an illness, an addiction? She thought back to that conversation and winced. What had seemed such sensible assurance then now smacked of righteousness since she had been treated to a glimpse of what Anya had been going through with Peter. Could she, Christine, have handled it any better? She doubted it. Even now, her fingers itched to grab Peter and pound some sense into him. It seemed impossible to believe that Anya had endured this situation for so long without losing her mind completely. Christine almost hated Peter at that moment, and then she was ashamed of that, too.

"There isn't anything you can do for him right now," Mark said, interrupting her depressing thoughts. "He'll have to sleep it off. Why don't we go and have a nightcap in the lounge?"

For an instant, she was tempted. She wanted to regain that wonderful closeness with Mark . . . or try to, now that Peter had spoiled it all. But the thought of drinking anything nauseated her, and then there was Anya to consider. Reluctantly, she shook her head.

"I'm sorry, Mark. I really don't feel like anything now. Besides, I think I should wait for Anya. She was counting so much on the clinic being able to help Peter, you know. It's going to be a blow to find him here . . . like this." She looked at Mark, pleading with him to understand.

"All right," Mark said finally. "But there's something I wanted to talk to you about. . . ."

"What?"

He shook his head. "It's not the right time. It'll keep. I was going to ask you at the beach, but"—his lips quirked—"we were otherwise engaged."

"Yes," Christine said with an answering smile. "So we were."

Before Mark left, he took her in his arms again and kissed her lingeringly. "Are you sure you won't have that nightcap?" he murmured, with his mouth against her hair.

Christine wanted more than a nightcap with him; she wanted the whole night, and every night after that. But she couldn't desert Anya, and so she shook her head regretfully.

Mark sighed heavily, but he didn't press her about it, and as she watched him go Christine cursed herself for an overdeveloped sense of duty, then went to her own room to wait anxiously for the sound of Anya's return.

Christine was annoyed to find Carla waiting in her room for her. She hadn't seen her sister since lunch at the restaurant, and that had been fine with her. Because Carla had been so conspicuously absent, Christine had begun to hope that she had packed and left that afternoon, taking off in her usual inconsiderate manner without saying goodbye. It was an unwelcome surprise to see her when she came in, and because she was worried about Peter and Anya, Christine asked curtly, "What are you doing here?"

Carla was sitting in a tall, wing-backed chair, her hands gripping the armrests, an angry expression on her face. "I want to talk to you," she answered just as shortly.

Christine recognized that tone and sighed with impatience. She was in no mood for one of her sister's tantrums; there were just too many other things on her mind. "Can't it wait? It's been a long day, I'm tired, and—"

"I'm not surprised at that!" Carla sneered. "In fact, you must be exhausted."

"What does that mean?"

Carla's expression became ugly. "What were you doing on the beach with Mark?"

Christine stared at her. "I don't think that's any of your business."

"Oh, really? I think it is."

"What makes you so sure I was with Mark?" Christine countered.

"Don't try to hide it! I saw you coming back with him!"

"I'm not trying to hide anything!" Christine snapped. "And what were you doing—spying on me?"

Carla ignored that, as she always ignored questions she didn't care to answer. Instead, she sprang out of the chair to face Christine with clenched fists. "Mark is mine!" she cried. "I want you to stay away from him!"

Christine couldn't help it; she laughed. "That's a ridiculous claim to make, isn't it?" she asked scornfully. "Especially in view of the fact that he sought me out; I didn't chase him."

"Oh, I know what happened!" Carla shouted, her face fiery. "He went out to talk to you, and you deliberately led him on!"

"I did no such thing!" Christine replied angrily. Then she realized what Carla had said. "What do you mean, he went out to talk to me? How do you know that?"

Carla tossed her head. "I know plenty, believe me!"

Christine wasn't sure whether that was just a childish boast or not. "All right," she said evenly. "Why don't you tell me all, and get it over with?"

"Where do you want me to start?" Carla sneered. "With the fact that Joel Franklin offered you a job?"

Christine couldn't imagine how Carla had found out about that. "So?" she said coolly. "What does that have to do with anything?"

"Nothing much," Carla answered smugly, "except that that was the reason Mark wanted to talk to you tonight. Poor man—he feels some sort of misguided need to tell you that you would be a fool to believe anything Joel Franklin says, especially about a job."

"And what exactly does that mean?" Christine was trying hard to keep a rein on her temper.

"Well, we both know that Joel wasn't really offering you a job, Christine!" Carla said scornfully. "How can you be so naive? After all, the man is known for the number of mistresses he's had—four in the past year alone!"

That was a blow, but Christine was determined not to show it. "And how did you come by this juicy little piece of gossip?" she asked contemptuously.

Carla tossed her head. "Mark told me!"

"And how does Mark know? A crystal ball?"

"Oh, he knows, believe me! And when we saw you in the restaurant, and I happened to mention after you left that Anya had told me about the job offer, Mark knew he was just putting you on. It was just an excuse."

"I see. Rather an expensive one, wasn't it, if all Joel wanted was to lure me into his bed."

"He has all the money in the world! Why should he care about that?"

The conversation was taking on a nightmarish quality. Christine was beginning to get a headache, and this round robin with her sister was aggravating it. "Look, Carla," she said with exaggerated patience. "Not that it's any of your business—or Mark's—but I'm a big girl now. I can handle Joel Franklin."

"Fine! Fine! I don't really care what kind of fool you make of yourself over him. Just don't try to use him to make Mark jealous!"

"Is that what you think I'm doing?"

"Yes—and Mark thinks so, too."

"Oh, really?" Christine said caustically. "You mean he thinks that now that you have convinced him, don't you?"

Carla flushed, but her expression was defiant when she answered. "Oh, I know your little games, Christine! I've played them often enough myself. I told Mark you were just trying to get back at me, because you were envious. And Mark . . . Mark felt sorry for you; he said you didn't know what you were getting into, with Joel. He said he was going to talk to you tonight and prove it."

Christine had never been so angry. She wanted to leap across the room and slap Carla silly for telling such outrageous lies, but there was such a ring of conviction in her sister's triumphant voice that something held her back. Seething, she considered what Carla had said, and she had to admit that part of it, at least, might be true. The more she thought about it, the more convinced she became. Now she knew the reason for Mark's sudden about-face; now she knew the reason why he had followed her out onto the beach. Oh, he had wanted to prove something, all right. But it hadn't been about Joel. He had wanted to show her just how much a fool she was. Pity her! The gall of the man! She had the hysterical urge to dash out to the cottage and tell him that his egotistical ploy hadn't worked. She wanted to scream in his face and assure him that if he had been trying to prove himself the better man, he had failed utterly. How could she have been so blind? She should have asked herself the reason for his sudden interest; she should have been warned by such an inexplicable reversal of his feelings toward her. Had he ever been anything but mocking and sarcastic toward her? Had he ever indicated that his feelings for her were anything but indifferent? Had he ever demonstrated any other emotion than dislike? No, no, no. She was so furious that she could have smashed something.

"Are you beginning to see the light?" Carla sneered just then, her face triumphant. "Mark was just—"

"Get out," Christine said to her. "Get out!"

"Oh, you don't have to tell me twice," Carla said scornfully. "I'm leaving, all right. I've had it with you and your superior ways! You always did think you were better than me, didn't you? Smarter, prettier, beyond compare in every way! Mom and Dad thought so, too, you know. Oh, don't try to look so surprised, as if you didn't know. It was always Christine this, Christine that! 'Why can't you be more like your sister, Carla?'" Her voice was ugly, mimicking. "'Why can't you get good grades, or get a job, or help around the house, like Christine does, Carla?' Oh, I heard it all, over and over, like a broken record, until I was sick of it!"

Carla advanced on her, eyes like slits, mouth a

bitter slash. "But I'll tell you something, Christine. I *never* wanted to be like you. And you know why?"

Christine couldn't answer. As angry as she was, she didn't want to believe that her sister could hate her as much as she seemed to now. She was too shocked to speak.

"I never wanted to be like you, Christine, because you don't know who you are. You're so busy trying to be perfect that you're nothing but a mirror. An empty reflection that only fills up when you try to be what you think everyone else wants. You're afraid, Christine—afraid to be anything but what you think you should be. Dear, sweet little Christine—always so helpful, always running around doing everything right. You make me sick!"

Carla started to brush by her toward the door. With a great effort, Christine made herself reach out to stop her. "Then why did you come here?"

Carla shook her off. "You know, I'm not really sure of that myself." She laughed harshly. "I guess I hoped—I really hoped—that what had happened at the agency was true. That you *had* gone to bed with that guy to get ahead. It would have made you realize that you're just like the rest of us, wrinkles and pimples and all. It might have knocked you off that damn pedestal you climbed on so many years ago."

"Carla—"

"Oh, forget it, Christine! I hoped that you might have cracked a little. Enough to be almost human, instead of Little Miss Perfect. Fat chance of that, right? You've had that mask of yours too firmly in place to change now!"

"Carla!"

But her sister refused to listen. "As I said, I'm going," she stated flatly. "And I'm going to take Mark with me, if I can. Goodbye, Christine. Run along and do all the things you're supposed to do. *I'm* going to do what I *want*."

The door slammed behind her. Christine was very still for a moment, and then she jerked forward, intending to go after Carla. As furious as she was, as hurt as she was by what her sister had said to her, she didn't want Carla to leave this way. Her hand was on the doorknob, but at just that instant, the phone rang.

Chapter Ten

Christine stood there, startled into immobility by the shrill ring. She looked over her shoulder at the telephone, her expression blank, as if she had never seen it before. The instrument rang again, insistently, demanding to be answered, and Christine shook her head. She couldn't talk to anyone now; she had to go after Carla.

But what if it was Anya?

"I can't stand it!" Christine cried angrily. Why did everything have to happen at once? She couldn't ignore the phone, and she couldn't rush after her sister, who would probably refuse to talk to her, anyway. Her outstretched hand dropped. Everything had been said between her and Carla, she realized despondently; there was nothing more to say, after all. Footsteps dragging, she went toward the phone.

"Christine, is that you?"

Rob Sullivan's voice was the last she had expected to hear. She had been so sure it was Anya that she just stood there stupidly for a moment, gripping the receiver.

"Christine?"

"What? Oh . . . yes—Rob!" Somehow, she had to get hold of herself. "Rob! What are you doing, calling here? How did you know where I was? Is something wrong?" She was gibbering, she realized, still unnerved by the scene with Carla. She made herself take a deep, steadying breath as she listened to Rob chuckle.

"You sound at sixes and sevens," he commented. "Is this a bad time to call?"

A bad time? It was the worst time in the world.

"No . . ." she lied, trying to think. "I'm sorry, Rob, but things have been a little—confusing tonight."

"I gather the hostelry business isn't all it's cracked up to be."

"Well, let's just say that the on-the-job training is a little more difficult than I imagined." That was better. She was getting a grip on herself now, able to concentrate on what he was saying.

"I'm glad to hear that. In fact, that's really why I called."

"I don't understand." And that was certainly true, she thought dismally. She didn't understand anything about tonight; her thoughts were a whirling chaos.

Rob hesitated. "Well, I have to confess that I hoped you would be bored with the inn business," he said finally.

"Oh? Why is that?"

"Because I wondered if you had thought any more about coming back to work at the agency."

Christine wanted to tell him that she hadn't thought about it at all. But besides sounding ungracious, that wouldn't be true. She *had* thought about it, more than once.

"Why?" she asked cautiously.

"We really do need you here, Christine. I mean that."

"Why?" she asked again. "There are copywriters by the dozens out there. And every one of them clamoring for the chance of becoming a group head."

"Yes, that's true. But there's only one that we—Richard and I—want to be creative director."

Christine was silent at that, too stunned to say anything. Finally, she managed, "But that's *your* job!"

"Not anymore," Rob said cheerfully. "Not if you want it."

Christine collapsed into a nearby chair, gripping the receiver tightly to her ear. Creative director? She couldn't believe it.

"That's quite an offer, Rob," she said at last.

"Well, you deserve it."

"And what prompted this?" she asked dryly. "In the normal run of things, it would have taken me years to work my way up to that—if ever."

"Oh, it wouldn't have taken you that long, and you know it. You're capable of the job right now—have been, in fact, for some time. It was just a matter of the right slot opening up. That, and me deciding to get myself in gear and go to New York to open another agency."

"You're going to New York?" Christine was surprised. Rob Sullivan was San Francisco to the core.

He chuckled again. "In a roundabout way, yes. Maybe. I haven't decided for sure yet. It could be Boston or Philadelphia or Miami. Cindy and I . . ." He hesitated. Cindy was his wife, a restless society butterfly who was given to extravagant parties and ruinous shopping sprees. Their marriage had been in trouble for some time, and that was one reason, Christine supposed, why the rumored affair about her and Rob hadn't been so difficult to believe. "Cindy and I," Rob repeated after an uncomfortable pause, "need a change. Maybe . . ."

He let the sentence hang, and Christine wasn't sure what to say.

"Anyway," Rob continued more briskly after a moment, "the agency is going to need a new creative director when I leave, and we think you're it."

"We?" said Christine carefully. "What about Mr. McLean?"

"He was the one who suggested your name."

I'll bet, Christine thought. If he had been so enthusiastic about her return, why wasn't he the one who had called?

"Well, what do you say, Christine?"

"I'll have to think about it, Rob."

"I understand. There's no rush; I won't be leaving for several months yet. But if you do decide in favor—and I hope you do—we'd like you back as soon as possible. We could work together for a while, so that the transition will be easier for you when I do leave."

Christine was cautiously neutral when she said goodbye. She promised to get in touch with Rob as soon as she made her decision, and her face was thoughtful when she replaced the receiver. She was more than surprised at Rob's offer; she was stunned. Creative director. If she accepted, she would be responsible for the entire Creative Department at the agency, answerable only to the president himself, who was, unfortunately, Richard McLean.

Grimacing at that last thought, Christine sat back and tapped her fingers on the arm of the chair. Could she work with—and for—Richard McLean again? Did she even want to try? Was the offer tempting enough to make her forget her aversion to him?

Christine Winters, creative director. It was a title she had worked toward all her years at the agency. That job had been her goal from the first day she had walked through the door. And now that it was within reach, that it had been literally dropped into her lap, a ripe peach, did she still want it?

Yes . . . No . . . She didn't know. Would she be a fool to refuse it? Or more of a fool if she didn't?

She wasn't sure of that, either. The questions buzzed in her mind, demanding answers she wasn't prepared to give, and in the midst of it all, another thought occurred suddenly to her.

Where was Anya?

Glancing at her watch, she saw that it was after eleven. Anya had said she would be back before now; she had to get an early start in the morning for Los Angeles. Christine knew that she had planned on packing tonight, and it was already late.

Then Christine had another unwelcome thought. Anya didn't have to dash back to the clinic, after all, for Peter. He was here, downstairs, sleeping it off, and how she was going to tell Anya about *that* scene, Christine didn't know. She would just have to think of something when Anya came home.

If she came home, Christine thought irritably. Anya was perfectly capable of forgetting the time, realizing it was too late to start back to Wheel House or that she was too tired to drive, and then deciding to bunk down with her friends. She had done that so often in college that eventually Christine had stopped worrying about where she was. She had spent too many sleepless nights wondering if Anya was all right —if she was sick, or hurt—only to discover early the next morning when Anya rushed back to the college that Anya had blithely decided to stay overnight somewhere and had forgotten to call.

But tonight was different, Christine thought with annoyance. She just couldn't go to bed and let Anya deal with the situation downstairs alone when she came home. Anya had been under too much of a strain with Peter; if she needed someone to talk to, Christine should be there.

Preoccupied with these thoughts, Christine realized suddenly that she had been half listening to the sound of the phone ringing downstairs for some time. Her room was directly over the

Lyle apartment, and she could hear the monotonous, insistent buzz through the floor.

She frowned. If it was someone for the inn, the service would have picked it up, since the switchboard closed at ten. Anya sometimes had calls routed to her apartment, Christine knew, but she wouldn't have done that tonight, knowing that she wouldn't be home to answer if anyone called. If it was Anya herself phoning, she would use the number for this suite, Christine mused; she certainly wouldn't call her own apartment, hoping Christine would be there.

Friends? That was a possibility, Christine thought, but again it seemed unlikely, since Anya had told everyone she would be in Los Angeles.

As Christine pondered, the ringing stopped abruptly, cut off in the middle of a signal. Christine felt herself relax, and was only then aware of how tense she had been, listening to that insistent buzz. What was the matter with her? If something was really wrong, wouldn't Anya have called her here?

The phone below exploded into sound again, making her jump. This time she didn't hesitate. Without consciously deciding it, she was racing down the stairs to the Lyle apartment to answer. Peter was obviously in no condition to talk to anyone, and as Christine opened the door she tried to get control of herself. Why was she so suddenly, so unreasonably, scared?

"Is this the Wheel House Inn?"

The voice was brisk, detached, and Christine thought with relief that it was some prospective guest who had somehow persuaded the answering service to ring through.

"Yes, it is," she answered. "May I help you?"

"I would like to speak to Mr. Lyle, please."

Christine glanced toward the couch. Peter was stirring, trying to sit up, his hand to his head, disturbed—finally—by the noise.

"I'm sorry, Mr. Lyle can't come to the phone right now," she said. "I'm Christine Winters, acting as manager while Mrs. Lyle is away. Is there something I can do for you?"

The man at the other end hesitated, and once again Christine felt that unreasoning stab of alarm.

"Miss Winters, do you have any idea where we can reach Mr. Lyle?" he said finally.

The clinic, she thought; it must be one of the doctors at the clinic. But before she could explain about Peter, the voice was continuing, and Christine felt the icy fingers of dread clutching her heart.

"This is the Mendocino County Sheriff's Department," the dispassionate voice said. "I'm afraid there's been an accident, and we have to talk to Mr. Lyle."

Christine discovered that she was gripping the receiver so tightly that her fingers hurt. Forcing herself to be calm, she managed to ask, "What kind of accident? Is Anya—Mrs. Lyle—involved?"

"I'm afraid so." There was a faint reluctance in the officer's voice, and that scared Christine even more than his neutrality before.

"Please," she said, and tried to stop her voice

from shaking. "Tell me. I'll relay the message to Mr. Lyle."

"The car she was driving impacted with another on U.S. One, just north of Mendocino," the officer said. "Both drivers have been taken by ambulance to the hospital in Fort Bragg."

Christine felt lightheaded. She swayed a little, took a fierce grip on herself, and tried to speak. "How . . . bad . . . is it?" she asked through stiff lips. She tried to shut her mind against hideous images of Anya, broken and bleeding on the road, and made herself concentrate on what the officer was telling her. Across the room, Peter had staggered to a sitting position on the couch and was staring blearily at her. If he goes after a drink, Christine thought fiercely, I'll kill him with my bare hands.

The man hesitated again. "Miss Winters, if there's any way we can get in touch with Mr. Lyle—"

"Is Anya dead? Is she dead?" Christine heard the shrill note in her voice, but was unable to control it.

"No, there were no fatalities, Miss Winters," the officer replied hastily. "But—"

"Mr. Lyle and I will leave for the hospital immediately," Christine said, hanging on to hysteria by a thread. She crashed the phone down without waiting for an answer and turned toward Peter, her face white, her eyes wide with horror.

"There's been an accident," she said, trying to speak calmly when she felt like shrieking out of control. "Anya is hurt. We have to go to the hospital in Fort Bragg."

"Anya . . . hurt?"

Peter stared uncomprehendingly at her, trying to understand what she had said.

"Yes, you stupid man!" Christine cried, rushing across the room. "Anya's been in an accident; can't you understand simple English? We have to leave—now!"

She grabbed Peter's arm and hauled him to his feet. When he staggered, she held him fiercely upright. "My car is in front—the Porsche," she shouted at him. "Get out there while I find the keys. We have to hurry!"

She didn't wait for him to answer, but pushed him roughly toward the door. Running past him, she raced upstairs, glanced wildly around for her purse, grabbed it, and fumbled inside to make sure the keys were there. Her heart was hammering so hard that she was gasping, and she made herself stand still. Taking a deep breath, she ordered herself to calm down.

Christine ran down the stairs again to the car. Peter was waiting beside it, just standing there with one hand on the door handle, pulling at it. He didn't seem to realize the car was locked, and Christine cried out impatiently as she raced around to the passenger side.

Her hands were shaking so badly that she couldn't insert the key. She fumbled with it, jabbing away fiercely, lost her grip and dropped the key ring.

"Oh, *damn!*" she cried, nearly in tears.

"Here, let me. . . ."

Mark materialized out of the darkness, reached down, and picked up the keys. "What is it?" he asked, unlocking the door.

Christine turned to him. "It's Anya," she gasped. "There's been an accident. We have to go to the hospital."

Mark didn't hesitate. He jerked the door open and said, "I'll drive. You're in no condition to do it."

"But—"

"Get in."

Almost forcibly, he grabbed Peter and shoved him into the back seat. The space was small, and Peter sat awkwardly, his legs jammed sideways across the seat.

"I'll sit in back," Christine said hysterically. "There isn't enough room—"

"He'll manage. Get in."

Christine didn't protest further. She threw herself into the passenger seat while Mark hurried around to the other side. He started the engine with a roar, and as they spun around in the driveway Christine clutched his arm. "Hurry," she pleaded. "Oh, Mark—hurry!"

Mark nodded grimly. "Hold on," he said, and floored the accelerator. With a spray of gravel, he headed the Porsche toward the coast highway.

Christine wasn't sure how fast Mark drove to the hospital. It was twenty miles, and more, to Fort Bragg, and during that entire time she took her eyes off the road only once, and then to glance briefly back at Peter. He was huddled in the seat, his hands clasped tightly together, staring out blindly. In the faint light from the dashboard, his face was just a pale oval, but he looked miserable. He hadn't said a word since getting into the car; none of them had.

Mark was concentrating on his driving, and Christine sat beside him, taut with worry, despising Peter more with every turn in the road. But when she looked back at him and saw how awful he looked, she was ashamed of herself. He was just as worried about Anya as she was, and she reached out and touched his arm in a gesture of support. He put his fingers over hers and squeezed them gently; she could feel him trembling.

"Peter?" she said softly. "Are you all right?"

He nodded, shuddering, and Christine saw that tears were running down his face. He was weeping soundlessly, and Christine felt helpless. She turned around in the seat again, trying to give him what little privacy there was in the close confines of the car. Mark glanced at her, and she shook her head. They drove on silently, and Christine tried not to imagine all the terrible things that could have happened to Anya. The road seemed endless.

The emergency room was quiet when they finally got there. Leaving Mark to park the car, Christine and Peter rushed inside. The place was empty, and they both stood there indecisively, trying to orient themselves. Christine had imagined frenzied activity; the silence and the quiet were unnerving. She glanced at Peter and he looked blankly back, his face a ghastly pale mask in the harsh fluorescents. Nervously, he ran a hand through his already disheveled hair. He looked sick, near collapse.

There was a nurses' station ahead, and Christine started toward it. Her footsteps echoed hollowly on the tile floor, and a nurse looked up at their approach. She had been reading a chart, and when she snapped the cover shut, the metallic noise made them both jump.

"May I help you?" the nurse said pleasantly. She was wearing a name tag that read Margaret Whelan, R.N.

Christine began to answer, but to her surprise, Peter stepped forward. "My wife—Anya Lyle—was in a car accident," he said hoarsely. "The police told us she was brought here."

"Oh . . . Are you Mr. Lyle?" the nurse asked professionally.

"Yes, I am. Is my wife all right?"

Christine couldn't believe that this was the same man who had staggered out drunkenly to the car on the way to the hospital. Somehow, in the interval between leaving Wheel House and coming here, Peter had managed to pull himself together. He looked terrible, still in shock, and he was visibly trembling, but he was trying hard for control.

"The doctor is with her now," the nurse said. "He can answer all your questions. Mrs. Lyle is in room one-ten. Third door to the right as you leave the emergency room."

The door to one-ten was open, and as Christine and Peter approached they saw that Anya was lying in bed, IVs in both arms, a bandage across her forehead, and a huge plaster cast covering her right leg from thigh to foot. Her leg was elevated in a complicated sling of wires and pulleys, and as Christine hesitated in the doorway she saw that Anya's lip was swollen, one eye was rapidly bruising, and the rest of her face was absolutely white. A doctor was bending over her, and when he looked up at them and gestured, Christine motioned Peter to go ahead without her. She couldn't intrude at a time like this.

"Mr. Lyle?" the doctor said.

Peter entered, his eyes on Anya. "Is she . . . ?"

The doctor stepped away from the bed, drawing Peter with him. Christine stepped back a little from the doorway, but she heard him say, "Your wife is sleeping, Mr. Lyle. There's no reason for alarm. I gave her some pain medication, and something to help her sleep. She was shaken up pretty badly, but her injuries are relatively minor."

"Minor!" Peter exclaimed, staring at the dripping IVs, the bandage, the cast.

"We put the cast on because of torn ligaments in her knee," the doctor explained. "There are no broken bones, but I want the leg immobilized for several weeks. As far as other injuries are concerned—a few bruises and scrapes, and that cut on her forehead requiring five stitches. She'll be stiff and sore for a while, but that's all. She was lucky."

Peter nodded, dragging his eyes away from Anya. "And the other driver?"

"He was lucky, too. He lost control of his car, it seems, and swerved into your wife. But we released him with a cracked rib, some bruises, and a ticket for driving under the influence."

"He was drunk?" Peter swayed, his face sick.

"Yes; that's why he wasn't hurt more seriously. He wasn't really aware of what had happened until the police came."

"My God!"

Peter slowly approached the bed. His face was haggard; he walked like an old man. Christine, still standing uncertainly in the doorway, saw the disgust and self-loathing in his expression . . . and the guilt. She knew that he was thinking he might be that driver one day, and she felt a wave of pity for him.

Tentatively, as if he felt he had no right to do it, Peter reached out and put his hand over Anya's. He was trembling, and he brushed his other hand quickly across his eyes as he stared down at his wife.

Anya's eyes fluttered open when she felt his touch. She could hardly speak through her swollen lip, but she whispered unbelievingly, "Peter?"

"Yes; I'm here."

"But what are you doing here?"

"We'll talk about that later," he answered, his voice choked. "You have to rest now."

Anya closed her eyes. The sedation was taking effect, and she was almost asleep. "I'm sorry about the car," she murmured. "I guess I made a mess of things, didn't I?"

Peter shook his head, his eyes filling with tears again. "No," he whispered. "I'm the one who did that. Can you ever forgive me?"

But Anya was already asleep, her fingers curled trustingly around Peter's hand.

Peter refused to leave the hospital until Anya woke again. The doctor assured him that Anya would sleep the night through, but Peter was adamant. He was going to stay, just in case.

At a signal from Mark, Christine didn't argue with him. He needed to be with Anya, asleep or not, and though there was nothing to do except wait, she offered to stay. Peter rejected that too, insisting that he could manage alone.

"But I want to thank you—both of you," Peter said, "for everything you've done tonight. I know I made an ass of myself, and I apologize. It was just . . . well, things will be different now. Dear God, if I had lost her . . ." His voice broke. He made an effort to steady it again. "You can't think any worse of me than I do myself, but I learned a valuable lesson tonight; you have to believe me."

"I do, Peter," Christine said gently. She was aware of a change in him, and hoped that it would last.

"I just hope Anya will give me a chance to prove myself again," Peter said. "I've been such a . . . a jerk—"

"Anya loves you, Peter. You know that."

"I love her, too. More than I even knew myself . . . until tonight. I want to make it all up to her."

"Well, you'll have plenty of time to do that, won't you?" Christine said encouragingly. "Anya in a cast is going to be a terror. You'll have a hard time just trying to hold her down."

"That, and trying to prevent her from hacking the thing to pieces."

"You'll manage."

Peter smiled suddenly. "Yes," he said. "This time I'll manage."

They left him then, and as she and Mark walked out to the car Christine held tightly to his arm. "Thanks for coming," she said. "I don't think I could have handled it alone."

Mark put his hand over hers. His fingers were warm and reassuring. "Oh, I think you could have. You were upset, that's all. You would have handled it."

Christine sighed gratefully as she climbed into the car. "I'm glad Anya's going to be all right," she murmured, resting her head against the back of the seat. Suddenly, she was exhausted.

"It looks like Peter will be, too," Mark commented as he started the car.

Christine raised her head to look at him. "He does seem changed, doesn't he? I mean, you didn't know him before, but—"

"I saw enough," Mark said. "But maybe this shock will turn his head around, make him realize how lucky he is. It's not every man who gets a second chance, with a wife who loves him—"

He stopped abruptly, his voice turning harsh. Christine saw his expression harden, and knew he was thinking of his own wife. She wasn't sure what to say.

They drove in silence for a few miles, Mark handling the Porsche expertly, downshifting on the curves, never touching the brake. His hand rested on the gearshift knob between them, and Christine stared at it, admiring his long fingers, the strength and competence of his hand. He had beautiful hands, she thought dreamily—a man's hands, tanned and square and powerful. She was gripped with a sudden urge to touch that hand, to feel his skin and the muscles and sinews below.

Her glance went to his profile, with his lean,

hard jaw and hawkish nose, and she saw a lock of dark hair fallen over his forehead.

It was so relaxing riding in the car; her body swayed with the curves and turns in the road, making her drowsy. She put her head back and closed her eyes, enjoying the car purring under her and the solid, comforting presence of Mark beside her. She was almost asleep when she felt the car slow and heard the crunch of gravel beneath the tires.

Reluctantly, she opened her eyes. She had expected to see the inn in front of her, but instead she could just make out the shape of one of the cottages—Mark's cottage, she thought sleepily. What were they doing here?

"What is it?" she murmured, confused. "Is something wrong with the car? Why are we stopping?"

Mark reached for her. His face was illuminated by the dashboard lights, and she could see the hunger in his eyes.

"You ask too many questions," he said, and kissed her.

Christine felt something leap inside her at the pressure of his lips on hers. His hands went to her hair, holding her to him, as if he feared she might break away. She could feel those strong fingers against her skull, and even if she had wanted to, she was powerless to resist.

The sound of the sea was a barely heard background to his murmuring of her name, and as his mouth left hers to move across her jaw and down to her throat she strained toward him. All else was forgotten in the tingling sensation of his lips against her skin; she knew that her heart was beating madly under his mouth, and that he could feel her pulse throbbing in the hollow of her throat as he kissed her there. She didn't care; she only wanted to prolong this moment, when there were just the two of them alone in the car in the middle of the night.

Their position was awkward; the Porsche wasn't made for lovers. "Wait here," Mark said huskily after a few minutes. He reached for the door and was around the side of the car in an instant to help her out. Before she realized what he was doing, he had lifted her in his arms. It seemed the most natural thing in the world to put her own arms around his neck. As he carried her inside the cottage she buried her face in his shoulder, enjoying the scent of him, clean and masculine, reveling in the smooth texture of his skin.

It was the most wonderful night of Christine's life. Mark deposited her gently on the bed while he went to put a match to the fire. Christine watched him through half-closed eyes, admiring the width of his shoulders and the movement of muscles under his shirt when he bent forward to reposition a log.

Mark stood by the fireplace a moment, one foot on the hearth, staring down as the wood caught fire. He was the most handsome man she had ever seen, silhouetted like that in the darkness, with the leaping flames behind him. His thick dark hair curled around his ears, and the planes of his face gleamed in the flickering shadows, giving him a fantasy quality, as of a man Christine might have dreamed about.

But this man was real, and when he turned toward her again, the look on his face prompted her to hold out her arms, beckoning to him. It was a magical moment, and she felt like a fantasy woman herself.

He came to her, shedding his clothing along the way, as she had slipped out of hers. He stood over the bed, and the firelight bronzed his skin, gleaming on his powerful legs and trim hips, lighting the hard muscles of his belly and arms, touching his broad chest and chiseled face.

Christine caught her breath. He was so handsome, so *male*, standing there, just looking down at her. Her skin tingled; she felt on fire. When he gathered her in his arms, she shuddered at the contact of their bodies.

"Oh, Mark," she breathed.

He answered with a groan and pressed her to him. His hands were at the small of her back, and he sank down beside her. They fell back on the bed, facing each other, holding close. Christine felt her breasts against his hard chest, and she shivered again. She began to run her hands over his back, enjoying his smooth, taut skin and the play of muscles under it. His buttocks were hard and firm, his thighs strong and lean, his shoulders broad and powerful under her seeking hands. She wanted to touch every part of him, to explore his man's body that made her feel soft and rounded and very, very feminine.

This time, his strength wasn't overpowering; it seemed to complement her. She felt secure and protected by him, and when his hands moved over her, she arched against him. Gently, he pushed her back so that he could look at her, and she felt no embarrassment.

"You're beautiful," he murmured, his hand caressing the line of her shoulder, her waist, her hip. The firelight illuminated her skin, casting soft shadows in the curves and hollows of her body, and he touched her breasts, encircling her erect nipples with his thumb.

"So beautiful," he whispered, his hand following the contours of her torso to her flat belly, and beyond. "So soft . . ."

He bent his head, and his lips touched hers. She wanted to hold him there, to kiss him deeply, to press against him and feel that hard, lean body covering her. But his mouth moved down, along her jaw, to her throat, her shoulder, the swell of her breasts.

She moaned as his mouth brushed her nipples, and when he groaned and rolled over her, she opened her thighs to receive him.

They moved slowly at first, savoring the sensation of each other, and the anticipation of what was to come. But neither could deny the desire that cried for release. He drove into her, and with each thrust she met him, answering with a need of her own. She wanted to engulf him, to draw him deeper inside her. She felt that exquisite sensation building, gathering power and momentum, and she knew from the way his hands moved frenziedly over her that he felt it, too. They wanted to prolong it, to hold back, but it claimed them, overpowered them. They reached the climax together, crying out in unison, straining to hold on to each other and that almost agonizing spiral of pleasure.

Exhausted, they lay in silence, listening to the sound of the sea outside the cottage window, watching the flickering shadows the dying fire patterned on the walls. They were close, as close as a man and a woman can be after such joyful expression, and they fell asleep, locked in each other's arms.

Sometime during the rest of that short night, Christine woke briefly. Mark had covered her with the blanket, and when she opened her eyes, he was staring at her, propped up on one elbow.

"Mark . . . ?"

"Shh. Go back to sleep," he whispered. He put out his hand and gently traced the contours of her face with one finger, closing her eyes.

Christine smiled and slept again, utterly content. When she woke soon after dawn, Mark was gone.

Christine thought at first that Mark had gone out onto the porch to watch the sunrise. Eager to join him, she threw on her coat and went out herself. He wasn't there. Shading her eyes, she looked up and down the beach, deciding that he had gone for a walk instead. But the beach was empty, too.

Frowning slightly, she went back inside. She caught a glimpse of the Porsche outside and went to the window to make sure Mark's car was there, too. The Corvette was gone.

She couldn't believe it. Sinking down on the edge of the bed, Christine tried to assure herself that there was a perfectly logical reason for Mark's absence. He had gone to get the morning paper; he wanted to surprise her with a Continental breakfast in bed. There had to be an explanation—something they would both laugh about when he returned.

But he wasn't going to come back. Christine knew it in her heart. There would be no newspaper, no morning coffee. He was gone.

There was an air of empty finality in the cottage; she could feel it. Shivering, she glanced around. The ashes were dead in the grate; the weak sunlight seemed cold and harsh. Chilled, Christine stood up slowly. She began to gather her scattered clothing, her mind a blank. It was an effort to get dressed.

In the bathroom, Christine stared at herself in the mirror. She had expected her face to be glowing, her eyes sparkling this morning with remembered pleasure from the magical night before. Instead, her features looked pale and pinched, her eyes shadowed.

Resting her hands on the edge of the sink, Christine bowed her head as tears stung her eyes. Where was he? Why had he left without a word? They had been so close last night, so in tune with each other. It had been one of the most satisfying times of her life—he had felt it, too. Hadn't he?

He must have, she told herself fiercely, raising her head. He couldn't have been acting; she couldn't have imagined it all.

She thought suddenly of her sister, and she could almost hear Carla's shrill accusations ringing in her ears. She had forgotten the quarrel with Carla; Anya's accident, and then the night with Mark, had driven everything else from her mind.

But she remembered that scene with Carla now, down to the last ugly word. Suspicion and doubt began to eat away at her the more she thought about that conversation, and Christine frowned. Carla had told her that Mark believed she was making a fool of herself over Joel Franklin; that Joel was out for what he could get. Mark was going to tell her that Joel's job offer was a ploy, and that Joel himself was a man who collected and discarded his women at a whim. Was it true? Was she really naive for believing Joel—or was Carla only trying to make trouble?

Christine wandered back into the main room of the cottage again. She gazed somberly at the rumpled bed, seeing the indentations where she and Mark had lain together through the night. Had it all been an act?

She didn't want to believe that Mark had brought her here just to prove something. She didn't want to believe that it had all been some kind of ego trip for him. And yet . . .

How could she believe otherwise now? Before last night, they had rarely spoken a civil word to each other; every time they saw each other they quarreled. Did she really believe, in her heart, that Mark had been suddenly transformed into a thoughtful, considerate lover?

She could have believed it, she thought mournfully, if he had been here when she awoke. She could have believed anything, then.

But his going without explanation had destroyed her trust in him. It was like a slap in the face, a dash of ice water. Christine felt abandoned, deserted—betrayed. She felt like throwing herself on the bed and crying until she couldn't cry anymore.

Where was her pride? Had she lost even that in her need for Mark? Would she do anything to get him, to have him, to keep him? Would she sob her heart out like some unrequited lover, clutching the pillow where his head had been?

Christine stood there a moment longer. She had no desire to cry now, no urge to indulge in a melodramatic scene. Disgusted with herself for even thinking of it, she realized what a fool she had been—a silly, romantic fool.

She should have known better, she thought bitterly, than to have surrendered so easily to Mark. Hadn't she seen for herself how hurt he had been by Deborah? Hadn't he told her himself that he had no intention of getting involved?

But she hadn't listened. She had been so attracted to him that she had ignored everything else. She had followed her heart, not her head, and now she was paying for it.

Well, no more. She was through making a fool of herself over Mark Harrison. She was a grown woman; it was time she proved it.

Snatching up her coat, Christine grabbed the car keys from the bedside table where Mark had dropped them the night before. She closed the cottage door decisively behind her, and as she headed the Porsche toward the inn she didn't look back.

Chapter Eleven

*A*nya came home that morning, riding triumphantly in style in the back of a van Peter had borrowed from friends. She was as irrepressible as ever, laughing gaily and making jokes about her fat lip and black eye, swearing she had gained twenty pounds overnight with the addition of the cast. She wouldn't allow Peter to carry her inside, but insisted on using the crutches to manage by herself.

"I might as well start right now," she said, grinning lopsidedly at the anxious faces around her, "since I'm going to be stuck with this thing for two weeks. But I'll tell you one thing, folks," she panted, after negotiating the steps; "it isn't like you see in the commercials! Christine, if you ever portray someone hopping effortlessly around lugging one of these things in your ads,

213

I'll sue you for misrepresentation. This bugger is *heavy!*"

Christine laughed, but she was as concerned as the others. She could see the effort this was costing Anya, and her glance met Mrs. Mallory's worried one as they followed Anya into the house. Peter was hovering anxiously, and even Pierre had emerged to see if he could help.

Anya collapsed gratefully on the couch in the apartment, and they all rushed around, bringing a stool to rest her leg, propping pillows behind her, covering her with an afghan. Christine saw the perspiration on Anya's face, and her attempt to conceal her pain. Quietly, Christine turned to Peter and asked if the doctor had given Anya any medication.

"Yes, he prescribed some pain pills for her, but she won't take them. You know Anya and her dislike of drugs."

Christine did. The strongest thing Anya ever took was an occasional aspirin, and that reluctantly. "Did the doctor say anything else?" she asked.

"Only that she should be quiet, and I should try to make her rest as much as possible. He didn't want to release her from the hospital so soon, but she insisted on leaving today." His expression was wry as he glanced at Anya. "She can be very persuasive when she wants to."

"How well I know! I guess we'll just have to do the best we can with her."

"I'll tie her down if I have to. If the doctor said she has to rest, then that's exactly what she's going to do."

Christine was delighted with this new Peter.

Despite his unshaven and disheveled appearance, he had a determined set to his jaw once more. He seemed resolute about picking up the threads of his life again, and Christine couldn't have been more pleased for him. Or for Anya, she thought, looking across the room at her friend.

Anya had been watching them with a smile. There was a look in her eyes that Christine hadn't seen in a long time, and Christine smiled, too. Anya caught her glance, and they nodded together in silent communication. Her good eye dropped in a ghost of a wink, and Christine's smile turned into a grin. She forgot her own problems in a sudden rush of happiness for the Lyles, and she knew that everything was going to be all right for them now. They might have a long road ahead of them still, but at least they would be traveling it together.

And what of her own road? Christine wondered after she had excused herself to head back to the office. What was she going to do? Take the job at the agency? Go to work for *WEST* magazine? Strike out on her own?

What was she going to do about Joel? Or . . . Mark?

She hadn't seen Mark this morning. Since her ignominious return to the inn, she had deliberately hidden herself in the office. The black Corvette was back, parked conspicuously next to Carla's MG, so Christine knew he was here . . . somewhere. She didn't want to see him. She couldn't face him. She was still too humiliated by what had happened.

She hadn't seen Carla, either, since their ugly

quarrel, and that was all right, too. She didn't want to talk to her sister; she was still too angry with her.

And with herself. She had never been so indecisive, so unsure of herself and the direction she wanted. Everything was all a confused muddle in her mind. Either she had too many options, Christine thought glumly, or not enough of them. Maybe she should just throw them all into a hat and pick one at random.

A movement outside the office window caught her eye just then, and she stood up to look. It turned out to be the worst mistake of her life. Frozen, she watched the scene taking place outside.

Carla was at her car, unlocking the door. Her dark hair shone in the sun, and as Christine stared she brushed a lock of it away from her face. For some absurd reason, the gesture seemed provocative to Christine. Mark thought so, too, for he paused in the act of putting Carla's suitcase into her car to stare at her.

He looked so tall, so powerful and strong and sure of himself, Christine thought; so handsome in a white cabled sweater and jeans. Gazing at him, Christine felt an ache in her throat, and she swallowed back tears.

It wasn't until Carla threw her arms around Mark and kissed him lingeringly that Christine was able to move. Savagely, she tore the curtain shut across the window, trying to blot out the sight of Mark's hands on her sister's shoulders, his dark head bent over hers.

Christine sank into the chair again, her hands over her eyes. She pressed her fingers tightly across her eyelids, as if that could shut out the scene she had just witnessed. But the image was imprinted on her mind, and she couldn't get rid of it. Over and over, like some horrible instant replay, she saw them kissing. It was almost more than she could bear.

She had been right about him all along, she thought. She had hoped . . .

What had she hoped? Angry with herself, she dashed the tears from her eyes with the back of her hand. Had she really believed that Mark was someone he was not? That somehow, miraculously, he would realize that he had made a terrible mistake by leaving her this morning— that he had discovered he was passionately in love with her and wanted her always?

Christine laughed harshly. Her head was stuffed with fairy tales. Mark had made it perfectly clear this morning that he wasn't going to get involved; that was why he had disappeared. *She* was the one who wanted more; *she* was the one who had convinced herself that he would change his mind and run back to her.

Her mouth twisted in contempt at her ridiculous dreams. She didn't have Mark, she had never had him, and she wasn't ever going to have him. She had to stop torturing herself on this emotional merry-go-round and . . . and do what?

The deep thunder of an engine outside interrupted her confused thoughts, and at first Christine paid little attention; she was too deep in misery. She assumed that it was Carla in the MG. Then, when she heard another, lighter motor kick over, she realized that the dense,

rumbling sound belonged to the Corvette—
Mark's Corvette—and that the other, second car
was Carla's. She leaped to her feet again, just in
time to see the MG racing away, with Carla at
the wheel. The black Corvette followed. They
were leaving, both of them, and at the sight
Christine swayed, supporting herself against the
edge of the desk.

She didn't believe it, she thought blankly,
staring after the departing cars until they disappeared from view. He had actually left without a
word. She expected it of Carla, who never said
goodbye, but not of Mark. No; not of Mark. She
had been sure he would at least have made an
effort to see her this morning, to talk to her,
especially after what had happened between
them last night. She had been so sure. . . .

Christine sank slowly into the chair. She felt
as if someone had slapped her viciously across
the face. She was numb with shock. How could
he do this to her? Oh, she had given herself all
the reasons for his behavior; she had told herself
that his motives were purely egotistical, that he
hadn't cared for her at all, but had only been
trying to prove something last night. But she
hadn't believed it, truly, until now. Deep inside,
there had been a tiny flame of hope that she was
wrong, an aching, desperate need to believe in
him.

But now . . .

He had gone without a word, following Carla,
as she had scornfully assured Christine that he
would. She was too stunned even to cry.

Christine wasn't aware of how long she sat,
frozen with disbelief, in Anya's office. Minutes

ticked by, but she was too shocked to notice the passage of time or the activity going on around her. She was aware only of a horrible, choking emptiness. Again and again she pictured that quarrel with Carla, and she could hear her sister's sneering, triumphant cry, "I'm leaving, all right. And I'm taking Mark with me!"

She really had persuaded him to go, Christine thought, almost wonderingly; she really had pulled it off. It was impossible to believe, but she had to believe it; she had seen it with her own eyes.

Eventually, Christine felt another glimmer of emotion threading its way through that terrible shocked void she floated in. And once she recognized that emotion for what it was, she welcomed it fiercely. As she sat there, fists clenched on the desk, Christine began to work her way through a whole spectrum of emotions, from sheer disbelief to fury. She didn't know where Mark had gone; she didn't know if he would be back. The only thing she knew with absolute, chilling certainty was that if he returned, she wouldn't be here. She never wanted to speak to him again; she never wanted to see him again, or think about him. The only thing she wanted at that moment was to run as far away from Wheel House as possible; to run as fast as she could. She had to get up and move, or the rage she felt would surely consume her.

Chapter Twelve

If the flight to Honolulu hadn't been delayed a precious ten minutes, Christine would have missed the plane. As it was, the gateman was in the act of closing the doors as she rushed through, and she flung herself into the seat to the accompaniment of the rising throb of the jets as the 747 began its ponderous trek to the runway for takeoff.

Praying that her luggage had been put aboard with her, Christine buckled the seat belt and sat back, trying to catch her breath. Her heart was still pounding from the mad dash to the plane, and she was tense from the nerve-racking delays she had encountered on the way. Traffic had been abominable on the freeway to San Francisco International; parking had been a nightmare. By the time she had finally found a spot for the Porsche, she had only ten minutes to flight time, and when she raced into the terminal, she had been appalled at the long lines in front of the counter.

The computer had balked when she finally worked her way to the head of the line, and more precious minutes ticked by while the agents conferred about the problem. She stood there in a fever of impatience, trying to get their attention, and by the time the ticket was in her hand, the last call for her flight was being announced.

She had to run all the way down the concourse to the gate, and if the gateman hadn't seen her dashing toward him, madly gesturing him to wait, she would have missed the flight. The plane would have gone without her, and she would have been left stupidly holding a ticket, and feeling all her precarious control slipping away into hysteria. From the time she made her decision to escape to Hawaii, her entire attention had been focused on that single goal, and if it had been stripped away from her, she knew she would have fallen completely to pieces.

Now, as the plane began to vibrate at the end of the runway with the buildup of thrust from the powerful jets, Christine realized that she was still taut with nerves, and she made herself relax. Against all obstacles, she was on the plane, and in a few more minutes she would be in the air, leaving everything behind, flying to Hawaii, and peace.

Flying? Fleeing would be a better word, she thought. Because that was exactly what she was doing: running away. She had never run away from anything in her life before, but she was doing it now. It was a searing thing to admit, but she was going into hiding because she just couldn't handle it all anymore.

Frowning, she looked out the port window by her seat. The plane had taken off while she was wrestling with her thoughts, and now she was flying over an endless cloud layer, so dense that nothing could be seen below. There was only an infinite expanse of white fluffiness, touched with gold from the sun. It was a gorgeous sight, one seen only from thirty thousand feet in the air, but Christine stared blindly at it, oblivious of the beauty, gripped suddenly by the realization that she hadn't succeeded in running away from anything, after all. Closing her eyes against the stab of pain she felt, Christine knew that the only thing she had done was to remove herself physically from an unbearable situation; she had brought all her emotional turmoil, the anger and the hurt, right along with her. It was here with her in the plane, hovering over her, like a dense black cloud, mocking her, and taunting her with the knowledge that it was always going to be there because she hadn't the courage to blow it away.

"Oh, God!" she groaned. *"Why?"*

"Beg pardon, miss?"

The voice startled her, and she jumped, nearly crying out from sheer raw nerves. A flight attendant was leaning over the seat, staring at her with professional concern. "Don't you feel well?" she asked. "I could get you something if you're ill."

"No, no; I'm fine," Christine said. She realized then that she was clutching the armrests in a viselike grip, and that the attendant clearly thought she was terrified. Well, she was. But not of flying, or at least not this kind, in an airplane. She was more afraid of just . . . letting go on the ground.

"May I get you something to drink? A soft drink? Coffee?" the attendant asked, still staring at her.

"Coffee, please—black." Christine made a fierce effort to pull herself together. The woman would think she was a complete idiot if she didn't muster a little poise. She forced a wan smile.

Reassured, the flight attendant returned the smile with a bright, polished one of her own. "We'll be serving dinner in an hour or so," she informed Christine. "But I'll get your coffee right away. Would you like earphones for the movie?"

Christine only wanted to be left alone. She shook her head, and the attendant moved on to the next passenger. When she returned in a few minutes with the promised coffee and a selection of periodicals, Christine congratulated herself on calmly accepting a newsmagazine she had no desire to read. At least, she assured herself, if she had an open magazine in her lap, she could pretend to be absorbed if someone wanted to join her. So far she was alone in the row of three seats, but she couldn't bear any company. It would be too much of a strain to try to make small talk while her life was in shattered pieces at her feet.

It had been difficult enough to talk to Anya this morning, when she had gone in to explain why she had to leave so quickly. She had stuttered and stammered some ridiculous excuse about having immediate business in the city, and then had felt awful about the lie. Anya had been so understanding that she had felt even worse. If it hadn't been imperative that she leave before Mark returned, she would have stayed. As it was, she felt that she was abandoning her friend when Anya needed her most, and it didn't help to be assured that Peter could manage without her. Anya had pointed out that taking charge of the inn, and its invalid, might be exactly what Peter needed to fully regain his confidence, and how could she have argued with that?

Well, she couldn't have, of course, and she hadn't. But her guilt about going weighed on her mind, and that, coupled with the lie she had told, made her feel like a traitor. Especially when Anya had actually encouraged her to go.

"Don't think I'm pushing you out the door," Anya had told her earnestly. "But if something important has come up, I understand."

Christine had almost changed her mind then. With Anya looking at her so innocently, she had felt as if she were betraying a trust by not telling the truth. What did her own feelings matter if Anya might need her? she had asked herself. But then, selfishly, she realized that they did matter. She felt worse than ever, and knew she had to tell Anya the real reason why she wanted to leave in such a hurry.

"Oh, Anya!" Christine had groaned, throwing herself into the chair beside the couch where her friend lay, propped up by a multitude of pillows.

"I don't have any business to take care of in the city. It was just an excuse."

"But you said . . ." Anya paused and stared at her. "Something's wrong, isn't it?" she asked quietly.

Christine rubbed a hand over her eyes. "Everything is wrong," she admitted, trying not to cry. "I've made a complete and utter mess out of my life, and I'm coward enough to want to run away from it all. Now you know."

Anya had been silent for a minute, considering her. Thoughtfully, she asked, "Is it Mark? Or Joel? Or both?"

Restlessly, Christine shifted in the chair and avoided Anya's eyes. "I don't know," she confessed, too ashamed to tell all of the truth. "Both . . . neither . . . a combination of the above. Take your pick. And to add to all this emotional confusion, Rob Sullivan called last night to offer me a job. He wants me to come back to the agency as creative director."

"Creative director! That's wonderful!"

"Is it? I don't know about that, either. I haven't noticed that loyalty to the staff rates very high on their list of priorities."

"Oh, I see. The woman scorned, so to speak."

"No—the woman slandered."

"It's an important position, Chris. You've worked a long time for it."

"Yes, and ordinarily I would have to work a lot longer for it. The question is, why offer it to me now? Is it a sop to my pride? Or theirs?" She was relieved to distract Anya from the dangerous subject of Mark; she could talk much more easily about the agency. In fact, it gave her an almost savage satisfaction to be discussing it so calmly. At least there was one thing she could talk about without feeling that awful urge to break into hysterical tears.

"My! What a cynic you've become!" Anya said teasingly, unaware of the despair Christine felt about other matters. "Could it be that the agency finally realized how valuable you are and simply wants you back?"

"Oh, sure. I worked my tail off for them all these years, and now that I'm gone, they've suddenly decided what a jewel I was? No; more likely it's that a big client has suddenly decided they want me—little me!—to do a big layout, and McLean, greedy as he is, is willing to forgive me for something I didn't do so that he can get the business."

"So you aren't going to accept?"

"I don't know. I'd like to throw their offer back in their teeth. . . ."

"But you know that a year or two as creative director could lead to something much bigger," Anya finished for her. "If not at McLean and Sullivan, for another agency."

"What are you?" Christine asked irritably, annoyed that Anya had put her finger on the reason for her indecision. "My agent or something?"

"Just the voice of sanity, my dear," Anya replied airily. "You shouldn't lock the door behind you unless you're sure you can open another one down the hall."

Christine glowered at her. "And where did you pick up that pithy little maxim?"

"Never mind the sarcasm. The point really isn't the job at McLean and Sullivan, is it? Either you'll take it or you won't."

"How simple you make it sound! Why didn't *I* think of that?"

"Stop skirting the issue!"

"And what is the issue, since you seem to be reveling in your role as mother superior?"

But of course the real source of her turmoil was Mark, and both of them knew it. Christine couldn't confess, even to Anya, what had happened, and so, in the end, she had just told her that she wanted to go to Hawaii for a few days to think things over. And that she didn't want anyone to know where she was.

"Even Mark?" Anya had asked, innocently.

"Especially Mark!" Christine said flatly. "And if you tell him—not that he'll bother to ask—I'll never speak to you again!"

"That's a little melodramatic, isn't it?" Anya said calmly.

"I mean it, Anya. I don't want anyone to know where I've gone. *Anyone!* Promise me!"

Anya sighed. "You're no fun sometimes, Christine."

"So I've been told," Christine said evenly. "But that doesn't change the fact that I still want your promise."

"Okay; okay. My lips are sealed. Does that make you happy?"

Now, sitting by herself in the plane on the way to Hawaii, Christine thought about that conversation and tried to tell herself that she was doing the right thing. Anya had obviously believed that she wasn't solving anything by running away, and deep down inside herself, Christine knew that Anya was right.

She should have stayed, she thought depressingly; she should have made herself face all her problems right there, instead of prolonging her indecision by trying to escape from them. She should have waited for Joel to return from his business trip; she should have called Rob Sullivan. And, most important of all, she should have been there to confront Mark when he came back from wherever he had gone with Carla.

Mark would have come back eventually, she knew. He hadn't disappeared forever, for his bags were still there, and he hadn't checked out. Despising herself for doing it, Christine had made sure of that by asking the maid if the cottage was empty and glancing over the registration book. Mark had paid in advance until the following day, and there had been no evidence that he had changed his mind. He had just gone—somewhere—with her treacherous sister, and that was that.

That was that, all right, Christine thought angrily, staring in distaste at the dinner tray the attendant had just brought her. Mark Harrison was a part of her life that she was determined to put out of her mind forever. They had engaged in a brief, meaningless affair, and it was over. Finished. Instead of sitting here feeling sorry for herself, she should be grateful that it had ended before it began. Mark Harrison was clearly intent on avoiding entanglements, and nothing was going to change that. Their lovemaking, as cataclysmic as it had been, had obviously been simply and purely a physical thing with him; he hadn't been emotionally involved at all, and she had been a fool to try to convince herself otherwise. What a romantic she was, Christine thought, disgusted with herself for cherishing stupid, ridiculous ideas about Mark. He had promised nothing; it was she who had built up some absurd fantasy about him.

But no more; no more. She had gone beyond that feeling of consuming anger into a state of calm acceptance, or so she tried to convince herself. She was not going to call him, or ask about him, or try to see him, or even think about him anymore. The experience had been humiliating enough without prolonging it in this self-serving manner. She was just going to have to forget what had happened and go on.

She was on her way to Hawaii, she reminded herself, and she vowed to make the most of this impulsive vacation by putting her thoughts to work on more important things than dead affairs. She had to decide what to do about her career, about her life. She was through playing silly little games, and sometime between now and the time she left Hawaii again, she would have herself under control once more, on the track and charging ahead with all the determination that had taken her so far in the past. This was a new chapter, and she was going to make the most of it.

That decided, Christine returned to her meal. But the filet mignon tasted like cardboard, and the wine, when she put the glass to her lips, was vinegar.

Chapter Thirteen

It was her last night in Hawaii. Christine had been in Honolulu for almost a week, telling herself that she was reveling in the beauty around her, assuring herself that she truly enjoyed the sights and the shopping and the basking in the sun on the white beaches, getting a tan that put Californians to shame. Each day was a wonder, every breeze a caress, each night touched with velvet. It had made her whole again, she insisted. She was able to think clearly once more about where she was going and what she was going to do when she got there. She was herself again: confident, poised, determined.

Why, then, did everything seem flat? The lush tropical plants growing everywhere seemed like plastic imitations; the incredible sky only painted; the fleecy white clouds like dull cotton. Even the pulsing beat of island drums failed to move her, and the bora-bora, that exotic and sensual ritual of the South Seas, was only another dance.

She had taken a cottage directly on the beach, and night after night she sat by herself on the open veranda under the palms. But the magnificent sunsets were wasted on her; she never really saw them. Preoccupied, she would stare blankly out as the fading rays touched the sea with gilt, and the light faded from mauve to purple and finally to a soft black that seemed to mute the sound of the sea to a sigh. She was aware of none of it. She felt nothing but a vast emptiness that went beyond loneliness into a hidden part of her soul. Denying emotion, she forced her mind into ordered thought.

It was a time of introspection for her, a time of reaching decisions, if nothing else. That last night, she had finally called Rob Sullivan and refused the job he had offered her.

He had been surprised at her decision and unable to hide his dismay, and it was then that she knew for sure that she had made the right choice, about the agency, at least. He had been so positive that she would accept that when he realized she had decided against it, he was completely taken aback. Christine was almost amused at that, if anything could have amused her. But the idea that Rob had believed she would come dashing back, all forgiven, in a rush of gratitude only made her angry all over again at the situation that had made her leave in the first place. It was good to feel anger, she thought; but then, it was good to feel . . . anything.

"But, Christine," he had protested, "what will you do?"

"Oh, I'll find something, I'm sure," she said, unable to disguise her sarcasm. "I'm not entirely without resources, you know."

"Of course not. I didn't mean that. . . . I meant . . ."

He was flustered, stumbling over himself, and Christine smiled coldly. Suave Rob Sullivan, reduced to stammering. She almost laughed.

Rob managed to pull himself together. "Are you sure you've really thought about this, Christine? After all, this could really be a boost for your career in advertising."

"I'm not sure I want a career in advertising," she replied calmly, knowing that would shock him to the core. To Rob Sullivan, the advertising world was the only one worth cultivating.

"Christine, where are you? Why don't we meet and talk this over? I'm not sure you really know what you're doing."

She was impatient at that. But it seemed too much trouble to argue with him, and so she said, "I'm not sure I know what I'm doing, either, Rob. But it's time for a change; I know that much." Then, because she remembered Anya's comment about not locking doors, she added, "But I do appreciate your offer, and maybe, sometime in the future, if I do decide to enter the sacred halls again, I'll give you a call."

Rob was silent, unable to deal with this new, cold Christine. But he had heard that odd note in her voice, and he knew he wasn't going to change her mind. Not now, at least.

"All right," he said doubtfully. "But . . ." He abandoned that with a sigh and said instead, "Well, good luck, Christine—in whatever you decide."

Her call to Joel Franklin had run on much the same lines. He expressed the same shock and regret that Rob had, but on a deeper level, and Christine had felt at a slight disadvantage with him. Joel had, after all, offered her so much more than Rob.

"What is it, Christine?" Joel asked when she told him, as kindly as possible, that she wasn't ready for a relationship—either a working one with the magazine or a personal one with him. "Did I do something wrong? Say something to offend you? I can understand about the magazine, but—"

But he couldn't understand how she could refuse him? Christine might have been amused at that, too, if she hadn't been unable to understand it herself. She wondered idly if she were really out of her mind to reject him. After all, she told herself, it wasn't as if he expected love from her. Just companionship. He could have given her anything she wished for. But would all the travel and the clothes and the jewels and the luxuries have thawed her frozen emotions? She didn't think so.

"No, it wasn't anything you said or did, Joel," she answered, relenting. "I suppose . . . well, I guess it's just me. I really enjoyed the time we had together, but—"

"But you don't want to get involved—is that it? Or—" He paused for an instant, an odd note coloring his voice. "Or is it that you've heard tales about my lurid past and tarnished reputation? I promise you, Christine—"

"No, it isn't that," she assured him quickly, before he could make a vow he wouldn't keep. "Your past, tarnished or not, is your own business." Somehow, even that didn't seem important anymore, she thought, and wondered if anything ever would.

"Christine, where are you calling from? Maybe if we sat down together and talked this over, face to face . . ."

Or mask to mask, she thought briefly, and then was startled by the thought. Was it true? Had they all been hiding behind one guise or another, engaging in formalized rituals, like masked participants at a ball? She considered the idea and decided that it was true. Anya had been hiding her despair over her marriage behind a pose of scatterbrained gaiety; Peter had tried to drown his sense of inadequacy with alcohol; Carla had barricaded her vulnerability behind a brittle, sharp exterior. Even Joel had cultivated a suave, polished air to disguise a loneliness that flocks of women couldn't assuage, and Mark . . . But she wouldn't think of Mark. Much better to think of herself, who had worn the heaviest mask of all. Carla had thrown it in her face during a blaze of anger, but it was true: she *did* hide behind that pose of perfection so that everyone would think she was someone other than the person she was. Then, when her mask had cracked in her terrible need for Mark, she had run away, fled so that no one would see that the confused, frightened, insecure Christine Winters was really only human, after all.

She realized suddenly that Joel was still speaking to her. It was an effort to force her attention away from these unbidden realizations and back to him as he asked her again to meet him.

"I'm sorry, Joel," she said softly, still gripped by the force of her new self-awareness. "But it just isn't possible right now. Please try to understand—"

Joel Franklin was obviously unaccustomed to being rebuffed by a woman. "I don't understand a thing!" he exploded. "I didn't think you were the kind to play games, Christine. I thought—"

"I'm not playing games, Joel. At least, not anymore. I had hoped that we could still be friends—"

"Friends! I don't want to be *friends*, Christine! I want—"

"I think I know what you want, Joel. But I just can't give it to you. I'm sorry."

He was silent at that. A new softness had crept into her tone during the conversation, and he didn't know how to deal with it, or what had caused it. But behind that gentle tone was resolve, and at last he said grudgingly, "All right. But whatever else you might think about me, I was sincere about the position at *WEST*. The offer stands, whenever you want it."

"I appreciate that, Joel."

"But not enough to change your mind?" he asked hopefully.

"I'm afraid not. Not now, anyway," she

amended, and thought: Another door left open. Anya would be proud of me.

Joel sighed. "Well, it was worth a try, anyway. Listen, Christine—here's my number . . ." He gave it to her, and dutifully she wrote it down. Just in case. "I hope you'll call someday—even if it's just to say hello. I really mean that."

"I know you do. And, Joel . . ."

"What?"

"Thanks for trying to understand."

"I understand only one thing, Christine."

"Yes?"

"That's one lucky guy. I just hope he realizes it."

Pensively, Christine replaced the phone. If Joel had been referring to Mark, he had it all wrong, she thought sadly as she wandered out to the veranda. She leaned against the rail and watched the moonlight on the sea, telling herself that Mark Harrison, and Rob and the agency, and Joel and the magazine, were all loose ends that she had just neatly tied and put away. She had burned her bridges behind her, and now she was unencumbered, able to pick up new threads and weave them into a more satisfying life, one in which she was free to be her own boss, free to do whatever she wanted.

Free to strip off her mask and be herself?

The question vibrated in her mind, a scintillating temptation. Oh, to be really free, she thought; free of the need to prove her ability to anyone but herself; free to accept the judgments of others on her own ground—or to reject them, as she pleased. Free to be.

Could she do it? She could try.

She wanted to take a last walk on the beach, but she realized then that there was one loose thread she hadn't tied neatly, after all. Resolutely, she went back inside and picked up the phone again. Dialing without hesitation, she listened to it ring six times before there was an answer.

"Carla?"

"Oh . . . Christine." Carla had answered on a lilting note, obviously expecting a male. When she heard Christine's voice, her tone was instantly guarded. "What do you want?" she asked curtly. Then: "If you're calling about Mark, I haven't seen him since the day I left. He dumped me. And that should make you happy!"

Christine winced at the vindictive note in her sister's voice. "I didn't call about Mark," she said evenly. "And I didn't call to start a fight."

"Why, then?" Carla said nastily, recovering her poise. "Oh, I know—you can't stand it when something isn't resolved, right? You had to call and make sure we were 'friends' again. Clear the air. Apologize for all the nasty things you made me say. Well, we're never going to be friends, Christine, so just save your breath!"

"I called to tell you that you were right," Christine said quietly.

"What? I don't believe my ears: the great Christine Winters actually admitting that her vulgar little sister might be right for a change! Now, that's a first!"

Christine closed her eyes briefly. This was much worse than she had imagined it would be. Carla's bitterness was almost a living thing, a malevolent presence between them that she doubted she could ever vanquish. But she had to try.

"I'm sorry you hate me so much, Carla. But I guess I can't blame you for that. I've been doing a lot of thinking about what you said, and it's true: Mom and Dad weren't fair, always comparing us. But what you don't know is that they were critical of me, too."

"I doubt that! You were always the favorite, and you know it. You couldn't do anything wrong if you tried. Not that you ever did," she added sarcastically.

"Yes; I know. I was always too busy trying to be perfect, wasn't I? But that was because . . ." She hesitated. She had never told this to anyone before; she had hardly admitted it to herself. Even now, she wasn't sure she wanted to give such a weapon to Carla, who might easily use it against her in the future. But then she realized she had to say it; if she didn't, it would all be a sham. "It was because they always expected so much of me, Carla. I could never please them, no matter how I tried. Whatever I gave, they demanded more . . . and more. I couldn't be an attendant at prom; I had to be queen. I couldn't just get top grades; I had to win the scholarship. After a while, I was so afraid . . . terrified . . . of not measuring up to their expectations that I never let anyone see how scared I was, how unsure of myself. I . . . I could never let my guard down, because then they—or anyone— would see that I wasn't what I pretended to be at all. I just couldn't endure being a failure!"

Carla was silent, and Christine waited tensely

for her response. She had bared her soul to her sister, stripped off her mask, if only for a brief instant. If Carla threw it back in her face, she wasn't sure what she would do. But there was one thing for sure: she wouldn't regret her confession, for even now she felt the weight of years rolling off her shoulders. It was such a wonderful feeling of relief that she almost laughed aloud. Was this what it meant to be free? Why hadn't she stepped forward long ago?

"Why are you telling me all this, Christine?" Carla asked finally. There was an odd note in her voice.

"Because you were right when you accused me of being only an empty reflection—someone who tried desperately to be what she thought everyone wanted. I never wanted to admit it before, but—"

"You were never a failure, Christine," Carla said, her voice small. "Never! And I don't hate you . . . not really. I guess what I really hated was knowing that I could never measure up, either. Not to you—"

"That's not true!"

"No, wait—let me finish before I come to my senses again and realize what I'm saying." Carla laughed shakily. "This seems to be a night for confession, doesn't it? Well, if you can expose yourself like that—to someone you have every reason not to trust—I guess I can, too." She took a deep breath. "I really resented you all these years, you know that? Yes; sure you do. I've made it plain enough, I know. But the reason I did that was because all the while you were running around trying to please everybody, I saw you actually doing it. You could always do anything, Christine—and you did everything so well! How could I compete with that? When we were little, I was fat and clumsy, and you were thin and graceful; when we were in school, I was bewildered by math, and you sailed right through. You never had to wear braces and glasses, like I did; you never had to worry about dieting, or if clothes would fit you, or if you had studied enough for an exam. You always reached for the highest in everything you did, and you always got it."

"No—"

"Yes, you did. And when I finally got those stupid braces off, and talked Mom into letting me get contact lenses, and when I finally lost that baby fat, I realized that the only way I was ever going to compete with you was with men. I couldn't do anything else, but suddenly guys were interested in me, and what a joy that was! I might not be able to compete with you as far as brains or looks or talent, but I wasn't such a dismal failure, after all."

"Oh, Carla! What a waste it's been, all these years. I never wanted to compete with you—not really. I was too busy competing with myself! I'm sorry . . . so sorry."

Carla hesitated. Then, her voice low, she said, "I am, too. But maybe—" She broke off again.

"Maybe . . . ?" Christine was almost afraid to ask. This closeness, this shared communication between them, was too fragile, too new. She didn't want to destroy it by saying the wrong thing.

"Maybe," Carla said with a nervous laugh, as if she were afraid, too, "we can sort of start all over again."

"I'd like that," Christine said fervently. Then, because she knew they both felt awkward, she added lightly, "Or at least we can try. Why don't we meet on neutral ground, and go skiing in Colorado this winter? I promise to fall down a few times, if you promise not to vamp every man in sight!"

"Boy, you drive a hard bargain! How about if we agree the slopes are off limits, but the lodge is any woman's territory?"

Christine laughed. "Agreed! How about sometime in January?"

"I'll mark the calendar. And, Christine . . ."

"Yes?"

"Thanks for calling."

Christine replaced the phone with a happy smile. She knew the skiing trip would be a success, and she was already looking forward to it. It would be the first of many outings with her sister, she hoped, and then knew that was true, too. She and Carla had cleared away years of cobwebs tonight, years of misunderstandings and resentments. They would never be alike, never think alike, but that was all right, too. Who wanted a sister who was a clone?

Christine's step was light as she went outside again, walking toward the beach, still aglow from her conversation with Carla. Now, at last, she was free to think about what she wanted to do with her life, and as she strolled along, her expression became more sober.

She knew what she wanted, she thought; she had known for a long time. But, as she had admitted to Carla, she hadn't been ready to acknowledge it until now.

The advertising world had been exciting, exhilarating—an endless challenge with never-ending pressure and tension. She had loved being part of that world, as predatory as it had been at times; she had reveled in it, she had carved a place for herself in it. And because she had been so determined to conquer it, she had been good at it. Behind her mask, how could she have been otherwise?

But life at the agency had been like a steamroller, a force that propelled them all along in a mad rush to promote the newest, the most advanced, the latest, and the most improved. Creativity had flared, to be sure—but briefly, like a Fourth of July sparkler, dazzling and brilliant during its short life, fizzled and forgotten when another product demanded another sparkler. There was no permanence in advertising, no sense of order and direction, no feeling that her work, however valuable at the time, was lasting. Her career seemed to consume everyone involved in it—a giant maw that was never satisfied; a god who demanded the constant sacrifice of one great idea for another, newer, better one.

Oh, she had loved it for a while: the excitement, the razzle-dazzle . . . the challenge. But now she wanted something else, and her brief tenure at Wheel House had given her the idea.

She had felt a deep satisfaction and fulfillment in taking care of the inn; she had enjoyed the permanence of it, being part of preserving something that had lasted for nearly a century and would go on giving pleasure and enjoyment for many years more. She wanted to feel something like that again, and she wanted others to enjoy that sense of timelessness, of history and proportion. In a world of fast food and junk cars and paper dresses, Christine wanted to preserve the craftsmanship of the past; to protect the quality and care that made some things endure while everything else disintegrated and became obsolete.

That was it, Christine thought: what she wanted to do was find another Wheel House to restore, and another—a chain of beautiful old places where people could enjoy the peace and serenity she had felt at the inn.

Oh, she had had her problems at Wheel House; she couldn't deny it. But she had been able to think things over there; she had been able to try, at least, to find a new perspective. It was something she never could have done in the hurry-up, catch-me-if-you-can world of advertising.

And she had been responsible for Wheel House, too; she had to remember that. It would be different for those who came as guests. She would find one of those old country houses and restore it, staff it, and sell it to someone who cared as much about it as she did. And then she would move on, to another . . . and another.

She could do it, she knew. She wasn't sure how yet, but the decision felt so right that she hadn't a doubt. And if she needed help, well—

she knew, from her experience at the agency, whom to ask. You never did it all by yourself; if you didn't know how to do something, you called in an expert. And she knew plenty of experts. Advertising had given her that, at least.

Now she could leave tomorrow as she planned, Christine thought. She had no regrets or indecisions. She was excited about her new venture, positive that she had made all the right choices, enthusiastic about going home again. Everything was taken care of; it was all an orderly, satisfactory progression into a new future.

Why, then, did she feel like bursting into tears?

There was a stone bench just ahead, and Christine went toward it, telling herself fiercely that she wasn't going to cry. Eyes burning, she looked toward the sea, watching the waves foaming in the moonlight as the surf washed gently onto the shore. She could hardly see it through her tears.

It was a beautiful night, her last night in Hawaii. There was a soft breeze, and the air was scented with a special island fragrance. It was a perfect night for romance: the moonlight was a silvery veil and the sky was black velvet, studded with tiny pinpoints of stars. It was a perfect night for lovers.

And she was alone. Alone with thoughts of a man she had promised herself to forget; alone with memories of another perfect night near another beach.

She tried not to think of Mark, but the memory

of him was almost a physical presence there beside her. In her mind, she could see the hard planes of his face, the leanness of his jaw; she remembered the way the wind would lift his black hair away from his forehead, and she could recall his eyes. Oh, yes: his eyes. So dark that she had gotten lost in them; so compelling that she had surrendered everything to him, even her soul.

She couldn't forget him; it had been folly to think she could. But now she could only mourn for what might have been, and know that she had never really had him at all. No man would ever match him; no man would evoke the emotions he had. She knew it, and that made it even more unbearable.

Work, she thought: work was the key. She would throw herself into her new venture, never giving herself time to think of him. She would exhaust herself so that she would be too weary ever to notice this aching emptiness—or to give in to it when she did.

"Cigarette?"

She had imagined his voice. She must have. It was impossible to think that he could be here. She was afraid to move, to turn her head. If she had imagined him, conjured him out of her dreams and her longing, she wouldn't be able to withstand the terrible despair.

She couldn't manage her voice. She nodded her head instead. She felt as if she were suspended in an endless time of anticipation—as if the flaring of a match were the only thing that would let her breathe again. If there was no tiny flame of light in the darkness, she had imagined him, and she would never be happy again.

The match flared.

Christine could barely see him in the blackness under the palms, but there was no need. She knew every plane of his face, every line of his body. When he stepped from the shadows into the moonlight, her heart gave a great leap of pure joy.

"You're a difficult woman to find," he said huskily. "I had to threaten to burn down Wheel House before Anya would tell me where you were."

Oh, darling, wonderful, disloyal Anya! Christine would send her a thousand flowers for this. She hadn't kept her promise, after all!

Christine managed to find her voice. "And why did you do that?" she asked coolly. Her heart was pounding so hard that it was difficult to speak.

He came closer to give her one of the cigarettes he had lit with that blessed match, and Christine accepted it with fingers she commanded not to shake. She wasn't going to lose him, not now—not now, or ever.

"Because I wanted to see you . . . I had to see you again."

"Why?"

"Why did you leave like that?"

"Why did you?" She couldn't believe she was having this absurd conversation. She didn't want to talk; she wanted to throw herself into his arms. But if she surrendered now, there would always be unanswered questions in her heart, and she would never be sure of him. Doubt would be a cancer in her soul, and it would eventually destroy them both. She had to know.

"I needed time to think," he said.

"So did I."

He was silent for a minute, his expression somber as he gazed at her. "I see," he said finally. He looked away from her then, staring out at the sea. "I can't blame you," he continued after a while. "I treated you badly—"

"Yes," she said unevenly, "you did. I'd like to know why."

He looked at her again, hurt deep in his eyes. She wanted to cry out that it was all right, that she would forgive him anything. But she couldn't say it. She had to know the truth, even if it destroyed her.

Mark sat beside her. Tentatively, he reached for her hand. The touch of his fingers was like an electric shock, and Christine began to tremble. She wanted him so badly, she thought. And yet if she weakened now, she might never have him at all. He had to free himself of his own ghosts; she couldn't do it for him, no matter how she ached to try.

"I was scared," he admitted finally. He held her hand tightly, as if he thought she might snatch it away. "After . . . after Deborah, I told myself that I wasn't going to get involved with a woman again. I thought I meant it. And then . . . then I saw you that night, struggling with that tire in the rain, and I knew you were different. There you were, soaked to the skin, alone on a deserted road, trying to fix a flat tire by yourself. Do you know how many other women would have done that?" He laughed harshly. "Deborah would have driven on, not caring about the car, just so that she wouldn't get wet."

"Is that why you stopped?" Christine asked softly.

"Partly. I knew you could never manage by yourself, but it was more than that. I wanted to get a look at a woman who would try."

Mark laughed again, but this time with gentle amusement. "You were so angry that night, so defiant—"

"So were you. I thought you were the rudest man I had ever met."

"And I thought you were the most beautiful woman I had ever seen."

She was silent at that, studying his face. "Then what about Carla?"

"Carla?" he repeated, as if he had never heard the name. "Carla was a . . . a distraction, I guess. There was never anything between us— there couldn't have been. She was too much like Deborah."

"She wanted more from you." Christine didn't feel that she was betraying her sister by saying so; she knew Carla would have told him that herself.

"I know," Mark said somberly. "That's why I left with her that day. I thought I should tell her that I couldn't have any relationship with her, except, possibly, friendship. We went to Mendocino for lunch. She left from there."

Christine felt as if a great weight had fallen away. She wanted to laugh out loud at the sheer joy of it. There had been nothing between Mark and Carla; how could she have believed otherwise?

"Carla told me that you came out to the beach that night to tell me I was being a fool about Joel," Christine said slowly. She didn't want to bring up the subject of Joel Franklin, but they had gone too far now to hold back. They had both hidden too much; it was time to clear away all the misunderstandings. "Is that true?"

Mark grimaced. "Yes, it's true," he admitted. He glanced away from her for an instant. She could see how difficult this was for him, but she made herself keep silent. Her turn for honesty would come, and then it would be hard for her, too.

"I was jealous," Mark said finally. He sounded so embarrassed at the admission that Christine wanted to laugh again, but this time from sheer happiness. Jealous. Then she hadn't been the only one!

Mark looked at her again. "I really thought you might go off with him. After seeing you together in that restaurant, I wanted to bash his face in."

Christine did laugh at that. "And then?"

"Well, when I saw you going out to the beach that night, I followed you. I wanted to . . . oh, hell, I wasn't sure what I wanted to do. I just knew I couldn't give up without a fight." He grinned abashedly. "Sort of old-fashioned, wasn't it?"

"Sort of," Christine agreed solemnly, grinning inside. "Did you think I couldn't make up my own mind?"

"Never that! But then, when we came back to the inn, and Peter was there, well . . ."

He didn't have to continue; Christine remembered that scene all too well, and everything that had followed it. There hadn't been time for them to talk; they had been propelled by events over which they had no control.

"Christine . . ." Mark grasped her hand more tightly. "Christine, I was wrong to leave you like that, I know. But after that night in the cottage, I . . . well, I realized how much you meant to me, how involved I was. I had to get away, to be sure that I wouldn't hurt you because of how I felt about Deborah and what she had done to me. I wouldn't hurt you for the world, Christine. You have to believe me."

Christine gazed into his dark eyes, so filled with emotion that she could hardly speak. "I believe you, Mark," she said softly. "Or at least I believe you now." It was her turn to hesitate. Finally she said, "Do you know why I had to run to Hawaii? Because I love you so much that I couldn't stay. I couldn't bear it if you didn't love me, too."

"Not love you?" Mark said, pulling her to him. "I've loved you from the first. I was just too proud to admit it."

"Oh, Mark! What a lot of time we've wasted!"

He held her close. She could feel his heart beating strongly as she rested her head against his chest, and she sighed deeply. They had gone through the fire and had come out whole again, with no more secrets between them. She was so happy she could have cried.

"Christine . . ." Mark held her away from him

for an instant so that he could look at her face. "How would you feel about extending your stay in Hawaii?"

"I don't understand . . ."

Mark smiled at her. "Remember those shopping malls I told you about?"

She nodded, confused. What did shopping malls have to do with anything right now? Was he going to ruin this precious moment by talking business?

"Well, I'm not going to build them anymore. There's a wonderful old house here, just begging for attention. *Your* attention—and mine."

"A house?" she echoed blankly, still not understanding.

"A lovely old Victorian—the perfect place for guests."

She stared at him. "How did you know?" she whispered. "How did you know that's what I wanted to do?"

Mark laughed. "After your impassioned defense of Wheel House? It wasn't hard to guess! What do you say? Do you like the idea?"

"I love it! But—"

"I'm glad to hear that," Mark said dryly. "Especially since I already bought it. It's yours. A wedding present."

"A wedding present!" Did she dare to believe it?

Mark held her at arm's length, gazing deeply into her eyes. "I want to be with you always, Christine," he said, his voice suddenly husky. "I want you to be with me . . . as my wife, my partner." His hands tightened on her shoulders. "Will you marry me, Christine?"

She thought she would burst with happiness. Everything she had ever wanted was in his eyes, shining with love for her. She tried to speak, and couldn't; she was too choked with emotion.

Finally she said, "On one condition. . . ."

Mark's expression darkened. Just for an instant that look returned. This time Christine loved it. "What condition?" he asked ominously.

"That you promise me another house—and another one after that. We'll have a whole chain of houses!" Her excitement was growing; her face was alight, her eyes shining as she pictured a glorious future with him. They could do anything, as long as they were together. She would never let him go, not when she had come so close to losing him.

"I'll buy you a thousand houses, if that's what you want!" Mark shouted, hugging her tightly.

"Then," Christine said demurely, "I accept."

Mark threw back his head and laughed. It was the most wonderful sound Christine had ever heard.

"Oh, Mark!" she cried joyfully.

"I always thought," he murmured as he crushed her to him exultantly, "that you talk too much."

Their lips met hungrily, and they sank together down onto the sand. Just then, a wave crashed onto the beach, spraying glittering droplets into the moonlight, like thousands of sparklers that would never go out.

Silhouette Special Edition

MORE ROMANCE FOR
A SPECIAL WAY TO RELAX

Six new titles are published every month. All are available at your local bookshop or newsagent, so make sure of obtaining your copies by taking note of the following dates:

MARCH 18

APRIL 15

MAY 20

JUNE 17

JULY 15

AUGUST 19

Silhouette Special Edition

Coming Next Month

Tender Deception by Patti Beckman

After the crash, memory gone and
appearance altered, Lilly Parker began to search
for her identity and found Kirk, her husband . . .
who had fallen in love with the woman
she'd become!

Deep Waters by Laurey Bright

Dallas fought her attraction for anthropologist,
Nick, from the steaming jungles of Enigma
Island to the moon-silvered beaches . . . but
where he was concerned she knew she would be
easily conquered.

Love With A Perfect Stranger
by Pamela Wallace

One night aboard the Orient Express they
met—and carried away by romance, Torey
gave her heart. Now, trip over, Peter West
would leave her life forever . . . or would he?

Silhouette Special Edition

Coming Next Month

Mist of Blossoms by Jane Converse

Singing star Brett Wells was tired of being chased by women. So how could Carolyn tell him of her love when he insisted that they remain just friends?

Handful of Sky by Tory Cates

Shallie had to make her way in rodeo, a man's world, and Hunt McIver's help was invaluable. But the man himself remained a mystery . . . one she longed to solve.

A Sporting Affair by Jennifer Mikels

Alaine's heart never had so much as a sporting chance of escaping unscathed once she met ballplayer Doug Morrow, the charismatic pitcher who made it clear he would have things his own way.

Silhouette Special Edition

All these books are available at your local bookshop or newsagent, or can be ordered direct from the publisher. Just tick the titles you want and fill in the form below.

Prices and availability subject to change without notice.

SILHOUETTE BOOKS, P.O. Box 11, Falmouth. Cornwall.

Please send cheque or postal order, and allow the following for postage and packing:

U.K. – 45p for one book, plus 20p for the second book, and 14p for each additional book ordered up to a £1.63 maximum.

B.F.P.O. and EIRE – 45p for the first book, plus 20p for the second book, and 14p per copy for the next 7 books, 8p per book thereafter.

OTHER OVERSEAS CUSTOMERS – 75p for the first book, plus 21p per copy for each additional book.

Name ....

Address ....

....